A HAZARDOUS ENGAGEMENT

NewCon Press Novellas

Set 1: Science Fiction (Cover art by Chris Moore)
The Iron Tactician – Alastair Reynolds
At the Speed of Light – Simon Morden
The Enclave – Anne Charnock
The Memoirist – Neil Williamson

Set 2: Dark Thrillers (Cover art by Vincent Sammy)
Sherlock Holmes: Case of the Bedevilled Poet – Simon Clark
Cottingley – Alison Littlewood
The Body in the Woods – Sarah Lotz
The Wind – Jay Caselberg

Set 3: The Martian Quartet (Cover art by Jim Burns)
The Martian Job – Jaine Fenn
Sherlock Holmes: The Martian Simulacra – Eric Brown
Phosphorous: A Winterstrike Story – Liz Williams
The Greatest Story Ever Told – Una McCormack

Set 4: Strange Tales (Cover art by Ben Baldwin)
Ghost Frequencies – Gary Gibson
The Lake Boy – Adam Roberts
Matryoshka – Ricardo Pinto
The Land of Somewhere Safe – Hal Duncan

Set 5: The Alien Among Us (Cover art by Peter Hollinghurst)
Nomads – Dave Hutchinson
Morpho – Philip Palmer
The Man Who Would be Kling – Adam Roberts
Macsen Against the Jugger – Simon Morden

Set 6: Blood and Blade (Cover art by Duncan Kay)
The Bone Shaker – Edward Cox
A Hazardous Engagement – Gaie Sebold
Serpent Rose – Kari Sperring
Chivalry – Gavin Smith

A HAZARDOUS ENGAGEMENT

Gaie Sebold

NewCon Press
England

First published in the UK by NewCon Press
41 Wheatsheaf Road, Alconbury Weston, Cambs, PE28 4LF
July 2019

NCP 198 (limited edition hardback)
NCP 199 (softback)

10 9 8 7 6 5 4 3 2 1

ISBN:

978-1-912950-23-2 (hardback)
978-1-912950-24-9 (softback)

Cover art and internal illustration by Duncan Kay
Cover layout by Ian Whates

Minor Editorial meddling by Ian Whates
Book layout by Storm Constantine

One

Madis Defranthea was poking around the market in Greater Quat as she waited for the passenger boat to Brute Rock. A last minute expedition, partly to calm her nerves before embarkation, partly on a hunch.

The stall that caught her eye held what could only be described as religious bric-a-brac. Books and beads. Little god-statues, incense to light for them and burners to burn it in. In a tiny scarlet dish in front of a lidded glass jar of such deep green it was almost black, a lit cone sent up a thread of sweet smoke. Something tugged at her. She settled her current persona more firmly around her and moved close.

The stallholder was a large, dark person, with the kind of stillness that is accustomed to waiting. Her abundant black hair was done in elaborate coils, threaded here and there with scarlet and gold. Her clothes were loose and white with orange and gold embroidery thick on the neck and cuffs. She wore a stone the size of a baby's fist and the colour of fresh meat on a thick gold chain at her neck, and another, smaller but still of that same disconcerting shade, set in a thin silver ring on her left middle finger. She nodded at Madis, once, as though any more would have been excessive, perhaps rude.

Madis was impressed despite herself. Such a sense of quiet dignity, suggesting power held in check, was hard to get right. She peered and poked at the things on the stall.

"Please be careful of the jar," the stallholder said.

Madis snatched her hand back. "Oh! Is it... is that your god?" A

5

little pompous, a little silly. Probably no one was watching. Everyone else was almost certainly waiting for the boat. But it was far safer not to let the mask slip.

"Not mine, no," the stallholder said.

Her voice was deep, but quiet, forcing Madis to lean in to hear her. Oh, that was good, she'd try that voice herself if she could pull it off. She wondered what was *really* in that jar – she could see something shifting in there. "Then what god is it?" she said.

"A river god. Just a little one, but a god, all the same."

Madis let a little of her cynicism show. "However did someone catch a god in a jar?" she said.

"I don't know. I didn't catch it." *Good answer.*

"Why would someone want the god of a river?"

"Fishing." The stallholder paused a moment. "Or drowning."

Madis bit her lip. Something was definitely pulling at her sleeve. "I have to travel, soon, by boat... Would..."

"Fifty."

"Fifty?" The squeak in Madis' voice was not entirely faked.

"Fifty." The studied indifference of a practiced bargainer. "And if it is restless, top up the jar. But only fresh water, always fresh water."

Eventually Madis walked away, forty Nobles poorer and one jar of something or other richer, hoping that her intuition wasn't playing her false.

Normally, she was more confident that a last minute impulse like this would be worth it, would give her an edge, some small but essential extra, or just the necessary sense of luck. This time, the doubts had started almost as soon as she had let the coins out of her hand.

And she would have to tell the others – Alina, at least. After all, if it really was a god, however minor, it added an unpredictable element to an already complicated situation.

If it wasn't a god, Madis had let herself be fooled, and that *really* wasn't how things were supposed to go.

The passenger boat was pulling into the dock; the Baridine arms (red and purple lilies on a dark blue ground) adorned the sail and the livery of the servants. Madis' 'maid', Alina, was waiting for her, luggage piled about her feet. In contrast to Madis' lean height and dark skin, she was short, curvy, and pale as the moon, with thick black curls currently jammed out of sight under a modest servant's bonnet.

Madis hurried to the dock, more than usually aware of her ridiculous boots and obviously, verging on ostentatiously, expensive robes.

She was taller, darker, and at least twenty years younger than the woman she was currently impersonating, but the current fashions made everyone look larger and taller than they were, though her boots were a careful inch shorter than was absolutely the thing, and her paint a good deal thicker.

She dug in the velvet pouch that hung from her waist and pulled out the heavily gilded invitation stamped with the Baridine seal.

The waiting passengers squawked and fussed like a pen of fancy poultry as the boat was tethered, a gangplank laid down, and the Castle's Constable took his place at its head. His livery was very fine, until one got close enough to see the fading, patching, and loose threads wavering in the onshore breeze.

"My lords, ladies," he called. "If you would kindly present me with your invitations, then you and your servants may proceed aboard."

"Girl, where is my hat-box? Did you remember my evening scarf?" Madis fussed and chattered while Alina made soothing noises and a series of nobles, grumbling at the massive inconvenience of one of their servants having to produce a piece of paper, made their way on board.

"I can't imagine why they want us to show our invitations," a ruddy-faced woman in ill-chosen yellow velvet fussed.

"Baridine seems *very* determined to keep his wedding exclusive," said her companion, brushing off the sleeve of his purple coat. "Considering who he's marrying, you'd think he'd want as many guests as possible, to make it all look more the thing, but this is a very *small* wedding. Almost as though he's embarrassed."

"Well who wouldn't be?" Yellow Velvet woman snickered. "She's practically a barbarian."

Madis and Alina were the last aboard. Madis thrust the invitation at the Constable. "Here, I kept it myself, my girl there is *so* forgetful." Before he could do more than glance at the document, she said, "Do tell me, is the boat quite safe? It seems such a long way!"

"It will take us no more than an hour to reach the Rock, madam," the Constable said, trying to return the invitation to her. "We'll be there in time for luncheon. Now if you would take a seat..."

"What if there should be a storm? I'm sure I heard someone saying there might be a storm..."

The Constable glanced around at the clear, sunny sky and flat calm. "I assure you, Madam, we will be quite safe in the Castle long before any such thing could reach us. Now, if you would..."

"Oh, girl, my shoes! Do be careful!"

Alina, laden, struggled after her. The Captain ordered the gangplank lifted, the hawser was cast off, the rowers strained at the oars, and the boat headed out across the glimmering water to Brute Rock where Castle Baridine glowered over the bay.

The boat was crowded to the verge of discomfort. The usual jostling for position was, of necessity, kept to a minimum, even the servants saving their rivalries for disembarkation.

"You know the story of Brute Rock?" The speaker was a man of middle years, decked in plum-coloured velvet, and a large and excessively feathered hat. "It's *quite* fascinating."

"Oh, little gods, it's Lord Mendir," Madis muttered. "He trapped me at a ball last year for a whole turn of the clock, talking about the new carriage he'd just ordered. I nearly stabbed him out of sheer boredom."

"Any chance he'll recognise you?" Alina said.

"Under this makeup? Besides, his eyes never got as far as my *face*." She caught Alina's expression and laughed. "It was the Fantine ball, remember?"

"Oh, *that* ball. Ah, that was fun. And surprisingly profitable." Alina sighed. "I don't get the feeling this will be nearly as much of a laugh."

"The siege of Baridine!" A woman in dove-grey silks leapt in to Lord Mendir's monologue. "My husband's father, Lord Lavian, was actually there! Can you imagine how thrilling?"

Her attempt to capture the audience failed as Lord Mendir simply rolled on "Oh, this was *long* before the Glass Wars," he said. "That," he made a grandiose gesture towards the Rock, "is the Brute of Quat

Bay. A leviathan of great and terrible power, who challenged the Sky God, I can't quite remember why, some rivalry over a female perhaps – you ladies, always causing trouble, eh?"

Madis noticed that the jar in her hand was trembling. She lifted it up, and peered at it. Inside there was an agitated swirling, and for a moment she caught a glimpse of something that looked a great deal like a small, annoyed, piscine face, with fringed lips and glaring, ruby coloured eyes. So she really had bought something other than coloured smoke. "Are you bored too?" she muttered. "Calm down. I'll get you some fresh water when we land."

Lord Mendir went on, "....in any case, he rose up out of the waters to challenge the Sky God... Huge waves, storms, lightning, all that sort of thing, and... Oh, yes, very dramatic, you know... and as the Brute rose up in his pride he was struck with lightning and turned instantly to stone! And there he is! Brute Rock. So perish all who challenge their betters," he added, to a murmur of approval, or perhaps relief.

At that moment a sharp breeze whisked across the bay, fluttering lace and scarves and whipping Lord Mendir's hat from his head. It flew as though its many feathers had rediscovered flight, before landing on the water, where it bobbed jauntily. "My *hat!*" he wailed, as the rest of the nobles laughed behind their hands. "Send someone after it!"

"We've no dinghy, my Lord," the Constable said.

"Well isn't there someone who can *swim?*"

"Your Lordship isn't that familiar with Quat Bay, I take it?"

"What has that to do with anything?" Lord Mendir snapped, staring at his still floating hat.

Just then, something rose from the water. It was large and finned and a bilious shade of greenish grey, except for its teeth, which were black, sharp, and numerous.

The hat disappeared into its maw with a *clop*.

One slimy dark eye rolled towards the ship, as though marking it for later, and the creature submerged.

Lord Mendir backed away from the rail, swallowing. "Oh, well, it was not my *best* hat, after all," he said.

Madis glanced at Alina, who tilted her head, with a faint but reassuring smile.

Castle Baridine rose from the craggy slopes of the Rock as a stark, uncompromising set of walls, broken only by archer's slots and heavily barred windows. Here and there the blunt roofline was adorned with a frivolous, half-completed spire, or a scatter of fancy plasterwork. The effect put Madis in mind of someone trying to prettify an axe with silk ribbons.

The water gate was heavily barred and watched by guards whose armour and weaponry, Madis noted, were not in much better condition than their livery – although still perfectly adequate for putting a large, unpleasant obstacle in one's day. From the dockside a torchlit passageway, cut into the rock, sloped up towards the interior of the castle. After some jostling for position which almost sent some luggage – not to mention a lapdog and two servants – into the dock, nobles, servants and baggage made their way up the passage, excited chatter echoing oddly from the ancient walls.

The room Madis had been assigned was at the end of a long corridor, at the Western side of the castle, with faded hangings, a rusted window catch, a chipped ewer and a truckle bed for the maid.

Alina fussed about, twitching at curtains, arranging furniture (such as it was), and piling up bags and boxes.

"Help me out of this, girl," Madis said.

"Yes, madam."

The boots had a great many buckles – considerably more than were actually required, and the gown had a great many rustling petticoats and tinkling accoutrements, not to mention a corset that could, when required, be made to creak like a marshful of frogs.

The resultant genteel racket was enough to cover Alina muttering: "Haven't found any peepholes, only wards, so far, but a fair few of them. And I don't like the feel of the place. It's not a happy house, it's got my back hairs properly up. Whatever you've bought, I hope it's useful."

"It's a god. Allegedly." Madis stretched her toes. "Ayay, that's better." She lifted off the elaborately dressed wig that covered her own straight brown hair, which she kept close-cropped, the easier to wear wigs or pass for a man at needed. Being lean in the hip and broad in the shoulder helped with that.

"You bought a *god?*" Alina yanked on the corset ties so hard Madis gasped.

"It was an impulse. It's only a little one, supposed to be a river god. Could be useful. Could just be some sort of weird fish, of course."

"Dammit, I wish you'd asked me!"

"There wasn't time."

Alina finished tying the corset with unnecessary vigour. "Your impulses are going to get us all dead. Or worse," she hissed under the chorus of creaks.

"Alina..."

"At least *try* not to do anything impulsive at lunch, for the love of all the little gods. I'll have a look at your god. Fish. Whatever it is."

"You worry too much." Madis grinned.

"Someone has to."

"I'm more worried about that thing in the bay."

"Hah." Alina snorted. "My people fished in the Copper Sea. I've seen my Ma yank her catch out of the teeth of bigger things than that."

"You sure?"

"I'm sure."

The gown Alina helped Madis into was far more elaborate than the previous one, and so thickly embroidered it could almost stand unaided. The shoes that went with it – thank the gods, river or otherwise – were lower than the day-boots, and easier to run in if necessary.

Beneath the gown, the new corset was a miracle of engineering. Lockpicks, knives, a little sleeping powder for humans and a different one – with packaging that would allow questing fingers to differentiate in the dark – for dogs. Although she'd seen no dogs except a wheezing sleeve-dog or two.

Everything one might need to pull off an extremely cheeky robbery.

With luck.

Two

Two Months Earlier

Madis clung to the windowsill, the toes of her boots digging into the brickwork below. Above her head pigeons fluttered and fussed, though not as much as the woman in the room. How long could it possibly take someone to choose a pair of earrings, for the love of all the little gods?

Finally – after Madis' hands had begun to cramp – there was the sound of a closing door, and silence. Madis eased herself over the sill, and made her way to the jewellery box lying open on the dresser.

She was leaving by the rather less awkward method of the door to the stable-yard when a figure that had been lounging against the wall straightened, brushed at the shoulders of his extremely well-cut coat and said, "Really, Madis? Hardly an ambitious target."

"Arden?" Of course, if anyone was nosing into her business, it would be her brother. "What are you doing here?"

"I have a proposal for you. Rather more profitable than robbing some matronly bourgeois of a garish trinket or two."

That was not, in fact, what Madis had been doing, but she had no intention of telling Arden that.

"Nice inn," Madis said. It smelled of fresh herbs, good food and clean linens, and the public room rustled with silk and clinked with gold. She sipped her beer. That was good, too. "You don't stint yourself, do you?"

"Why would I?" Arden summoned a server with a flick of his fingers. "And you're staying in the Black Pig, I understand."

"*Must* you spy on me?"

"That's a harsh way to put it. I'm interested in what you're up to, little sister."

"I am older than you, Arden."

"You don't need to remind me, my dear." He looked her up and down. "It shows."

She forbore to comment. They both had the dark-oak skin and thick, straight black hair of their departed mother, and their father's sharp-cut features. Madis was perfectly at home with her appearance, but Arden never ceased trying to needle her about it.

The conversation paused as the server took their order. Madis looked Arden over as he enquired about the freshness of the fish. He wore a sharply-cut coat in the latest style, and a rakish hat decorated with a puff of dark red silk to match the coat's cuffs lay on the table.

"And what is this proposal of yours?" She said, when the server was safely out of earshot.

"Belani is retiring. She's met some ghastly farmer, and wants to live in rural splendour and raise chickens. Or babies. Possibly both, I went deaf with boredom before she finished chattering about it. So, there's going to be an opening in my happy little ensemble."

Madis almost choked on her beer. "You want me to..."

"I've a job in mind. I wasn't sure if you could handle it, but since you succeeded in Mithelden – really quite neatly – I thought I'd offer you a prize. I'm willing to consider you for Belani's place, if you can pull it off."

"And why would I want to do that?"

"Madis, my dear. You've been lucky so far."

"I'd have been luckier if you hadn't tried to muscle in on the Intivadi job."

"Oh, are you *still* peeved about that? No one got hurt, did they?"

"No one got any money, either. *And* we escaped arrest by a sliver."

Arden waved the past away. "You'd be far better off under my leadership."

She leaned back, stuffed her hands in her pockets, and looked at him. "I have a team."

"I might be willing to take on one or two of them. Perhaps." He raised an eyebrow at her. "You can hardly expect me to adopt every waif and stray you choose to work with. Even if they were up to it, I don't run a petticoat army."

"Apart from Belani."

"Belani had... other attributes. Ones I don't look for in my *sister*." He leaned back and regarded her with a smile that made her fists itch. "What do you say? Pull off this job, and we can work together. Like family should."

The fish arrived, beautifully cooked and smelling delicious.

"So," Madis said, after a few mouthfuls, "what's the job?"

"I'm sure the sausage at the Black Pig is perfectly adequate, but this deserves your full attention." Arden waved his knife at her reprovingly. "Take some time to appreciate it."

They ate in silence, Madis devouring hers in minutes and pushing the stripped bones around her plate until Arden finally extracted the last fragment and leaned back from the table with a sigh of satisfaction.

"There, wasn't that worth it?" He smiled. "And now, a little of the Desert Flower, I think. "

"Not for me." Madis said.

"If you're sure... You, boy," Arden said to the server, a man of at least fifty. "Desert Flower. And I want the twenty year old. Don't try and palm me off with the ten."

Once the man had gone, Arden sighed. "The service has gone downhill. I do prefer something pretty to look at while I'm eating."

"Are you going to tell me what this job is?"

"Not here." He threw a handful of coins on the table, and picked up his glass.

Madis added some more coins, gave the server an apologetic glance and followed Arden up to his room – the best in the house, of course. She stood by the window, peering into the street, while he sprawled in the large wingback chair.

"So?" She said.

"So. You've heard of Lord Baridine."

Madis frowned. "Something to do with the Glass Wars? Wait,

14

wasn't there some famous siege?"

"Indeed. Baridine Castle guards Brute Rock, and Brute Rock guards Quat Bay. Baridine has never been defeated. The siege marked a turning point in the Glass Wars. The King was very grateful, but unfortunately all that gratitude only led to a little gold and some grants of land that proved sadly unproductive. Lord Baridine died, his son came briefly into the inheritance and managed to spend much of it, before dying – of either drink or pox, or both. *His* son, the current Lord Baridine, has spent most of what was left. "

"If they've spent all their money, why are *you* interested in them?"

"Because Lord Baridine has had the extreme good fortune to find himself a very wealthy bride. One Lady Casillienne of Darnor."

"Darnor? That's somewhere in the north, isn't it?"

"Indeed. And the poor lady won't have any of her family at the wedding as snow has cut off the passes. Although that might be a relief, at least for the rest of the guests. Not only are they northerners, their money comes from trade."

"I really don't understand the objection," Madis said. "It's money. Unless the trade's slaving."

"Not that I know of," Arden said. "Metals. Wool. All terribly tedious but quite profitable. In any case, there will be an excellent dowry, once the passes open. In the meantime Baridine is inviting the cream of the local nobility to witness his nuptials."

"Don't tell me you're after the wedding gifts. That's a little low, even for you."

"No. I have a buyer for one specific object."

"What?"

"A belt. An engagement gift to the young bride from her betrothed. It's a magical focus; capable of intensifying the magic of a talented wearer a hundredfold, and currently attached to her presumably virginal waist with one very powerful spell and a good old-fashioned lock."

"A belt, locked to the waist of the woman at the centre of the attention of several hundred people, in an un-invadable castle, on a rock, in the sea."

"Too risky for you?" Arden said, brushing a crumb from his breeches.

"Why not wait until she leaves? Goes swanning around the countryside showing her newlywed self off to the peasantry?"

"The belt *has* to be removed before the wedding."

"Why?"

Arden shrugged. "The buyer demands it. I assume there's a reason. I don't pretend to be an expert in magical items."

"Did the buyer give you the counterspell, or does that have to be dug up too?"

"I have the counterspell. I'll even give it to you, free of charge. What do you say? If you succeed, an even split. Half for me, half for you and your team."

"That's an interesting definition of 'even'." Madis gave her brother a level look. "Me and my team take all the risks, and you take half the prize?"

"But without me you would not know the prize was there to be got. *And* you get to join my team."

"How much is your buyer offering, anyway?"

"Twenty thousand nobles."

"A tidy sum. So, brother mine, why aren't you doing it yourself?"

"You don't want the job?"

"I didn't say that. I just wondered."

"Because if I'm offering you a place on my team, I want you to prove yourself."

Madis chewed her lip. "When's the wedding?"

"The festival of the Evening Star."

"That's less than a moon!"

"I know." Arden rolled his eyes. "Inappropriately hasty, in my opinion – I assume it was the bride's doing. Typical bourgeoisie. No doubt she's afraid he'll tire of her savage northern ways and change his mind."

"How am I supposed to get everything set up in that amount of time?"

"Well, that will be a test of your abilities, won't it, little sister?"

Madis leaned back. "And if I try, and fail? Your buyer won't be happy."

"I don't get paid until she has the item in hand."

Madis sighed. "I'll talk to the others."

"Oh, I'm afraid I can't wait around – or risk word of this getting out. There is, as you pointed out, less than a moon before the wedding. Yes, or no?"

"All right! All right! Yes! I'll do it."

Arden smiled, patted her hand, and tugged on the bell-rope by the bed. "I think we should celebrate, don't you? And this time I insist you join me in a glass. We are family, after all."

Once she had finally got away from Arden, Madis went back to her room at the Black Pig, and sat on the narrow bed with her feet tucked under her, thinking hard.

She had not been there long when there was a knock on the door. "Lady for you, miss."

She got up and followed the tap-boy to the crowded bar. The smells of beer, cheap perfume, sweat and sausages thickened the air.

The woman who was waiting had a round, pretty face and tight dark curls. She flung out her hands at the sight of Madis. "Oh, thank you! Thank you so much! I don't know what... You must let me pay you, something, at least!"

"Hello, Jara." Madis smiled and put a finger to her lips.

"Oh!" Jara said. "Of course... I'm sorry... I'm just so *thankful...*"

"Come to my room a moment," Madis said. "We can talk there."

"Oh, well..." Jara glanced around, and nodded. "Yes. All right."

"So," Madis said, when they were both sitting on her bed. "It went all right?"

"Her ladyship never even noticed it was missing! I'd have lost my place, at the very least of it."

"I've met her ladyship. You'd have been in clink, love."

"Did you see Dobrin?"

"I did. And I had a word with him."

Jara's face fell. "You didn't... hurt him, did you?"

"I put the fear of the Sea Goddess in him, is what I did. He's no good for you, Jara. He didn't care what would happen to you when she found that necklace gone."

"No, I know." Jara sighed.

"You're not going to take him back, I hope?"

"No. This isn't the first time he... No."

"Good. I don't want to have to put any more trinkets back where they belong." *Or see you with a black eye because you told him no.*

The light of a lowering sun flooded the practice room, elongating the dancing shadows. Shouts echoed, the thwack of wooden swords hitting gambazons, hilts, and occasionally, shins.

The smell of sweat and leather.

Fourteen young men, sparring, chattering, lounging. A handful of manservants, waiting on benches at one side of the room.

Two tutors, one stocky, the other lanky.

A shriek. One of the young men dropped his guard and fell back, hopping and swearing.

"Enough for today," the stocky tutor said. His pushed-back helm showed a jowly, stubbled face. "Lord Colet, if that swells, I'd get a healer to it, but I think it's just a bruise."

Lord Colet, still scowling, gestured to his manservant, hauled off his gambazon, and threw his kit in the general direction of a leather bag on the floor. "I was *distracted,*" he said, glaring at the lanky tutor, who stood impassive, helmet still on. "I shall ask my father to find me a class with *proper* tutors."

There was a moment's silence, while the other young men looked at each other.

"Bavez, are you coming?" Colet said.

His friend ducked his head. "I'll be along later."

"Fool.*" Colet strode out. His manservant scurried to collect everything and went after him.

One by one the others followed, apart from Bavez, who was one of those young men who seem loosely put together, as though made up of parts from other people that almost, but don't quite match. He rubbed a hand over his mouth. "Did you need something, my Lord?" The stocky tutor said.

"No. Just... he's wrong," Bavez burst out, in the direction of the lanky figure. "You're *good.*"

She pulled off her helm, revealing close-cropped hair as furiously orange as the sunset light flooding through the big windows. "Thank you," she said gravely.

Bavez, blushing, muttered something and skittered out of the room, tripping on the step.

"Someone has a crush," the stocky tutor said.

"He'll get over it. This isn't going to work."

"Give 'em time."

"Numbers keep dropping, Danad."

Danad shrugged. "So we've lost a handful that weren't worth the teaching. Like Colet. He'll go from tutor to tutor, looking for someone who can magically turn him into a decent swordsman without him putting in any effort. It's a common enough with these sprigs of the nobility. They think they should be born with it like they were everything else, and get all pissbritches when they find it takes work."

"Even bad students pay." Milandree put her waster in the rack. "Time to call it. Don't want to repay you by ruining your business."

Danad opened his mouth, and closed it, and sighed.

"Well, you're a gloomy lot."

"Madis!" Milandree spun around, a rare smile lighting her face. "Danad, Madis. Madis, Danad. My employer. For now."

"A man of perception and sense," Madis said, holding out her hand to Danad, who bowed over it with the limber grace of a man who might be well into his sixtieth year but ran around crossing practice swords with striplings all day.

"Delighted to meet any friend of Milandree's," he said. "Now please take her off my hands and pour some drink down her until she cheers up. We've no pupils tomorrow."

"None?" Milandree frowned. "Danad..."

"Shoo." He flapped his hands at her. "Go with your friend. I'll see you in two days. And you can drop in at that lazy bastard smith's for me and tell him I want those hilts fixed before I fucking die of old age." He glanced at Madis and flushed. "Sorry," he said.

Madis waved a hand. "I've heard worse. I've said worse, come to that. Come along, dear, I'm under orders to get you drunk. I don't want to get you in trouble with your boss."

The inn was scruffier than the Black Pig, but the beer was good.

"I was sorry to hear about your father," Madis said. "And the schola. How did you end up with Danad? I thought the money from the last job would be enough to hold you."

Milandree shrugged. "Once Father got sick, custom dropped off. Not enough pupils who'd train with me. Couldn't keep up the rent on the building. Danad fought alongside my father. When I had to close the schola, he offered me the job. "

"You like the work?"

"Mostly, yes."

"You still want to run your own schola?"

"No point. Even if I could afford to start one up and equip it, same problem. Not enough pupils."

"What's *wrong* with them? You're the best fighter I know!"

"You know what's wrong." Milandree shrugged.

"What about women?"

One of Milandree's coppery eyebrows rose a fraction.

"I'm not asking about your personal life," Madis grinned, "as if you'd spill anyway. What about that schola for women? Not like you haven't talked about it."

"No one would come."

"I would. Half the women we know would."

"That's not enough to fill a schola."

Madis chewed her lip. "Damn, you really are gloomy today. Look, are you serious about leaving Danad?"

"He's been good to me. I'm ruining his business. So, yes."

"Up for a job, then?"

"Hah." One side of Milandree's mouth lifted slightly. "Thought so. What is it?"

"I want to wait until everyone's together."

"Everyone? Same as last time?"

"Same as last time. I think you'll like it."

"All right."

"Excellent!" Madis waved to the server. "Now let's get on with getting you drunk like I promised."

"Well, it's a good looking beast." A young man, dressed in the very razor edge of the latest court fashion, looked up at the gleaming black mass of equine muscle and irritation that stood in the yard; a beast with an arched neck and dappled flanks, and, currently, a striking white blaze down its handsome nose. A manservant in heavily embroidered livery stood to one side, his face carefully expressionless, holding the courtier's horse – a handsome but nervy grey with welts along its flanks – and his own, an older beast that lipped wearily at a patch of grass growing by the wall.

"You people certainly know your horseflesh – Dagri, isn't it?" The courtier glanced at the young woman holding the horse. She had a broad face and long, dark eyes under strongly marked brows and was dressed in a quilted jacket embroidered in scarlet and emerald, and trousers of soft hide.

"So it is said, Lord Galzas," Dagri replied. "And Shaikan is very fine, but headstrong. The chestnut mare...."

"What am I, a maiden bride? Chestnut mare, indeed. A soft pretty ride. No." Lord Galzas leaned towards the horse. "Shaikan. Hmm."

With a snort of fury, Shaikan bucked and lashed out. The servant staggered backwards, his face wearing the sweating-cheese expression of someone who has just felt a living war-hammer whisk close enough to brush his hair. "My Lord..."

"Quiet, man. There isn't a horse I can't break. How much?"

"Two hundred and fifty nobles," Dagri said.

"Not before I try his paces," the courtier said.

"As you will." Dagri murmured to Shaikan and patted his neck. He stood like a stock as the young man swung himself easily into the saddle, but shook his head and snorted at the first tug on the reins. Lord Galzas managed to urge him to a trot, but Shaikan refused to canter, balking and huffing. Eventually the rider gave up, yanked him to a halt and slid off. He sidestepped the horse's attempt to bite him, and tossed the reins to Dagri. "He needs a firm hand. I'll take him, but not for two hundred and fifty."

"Then perhaps the mare..."

"No. I want this horse." Galzas smiled. "I'll school him, soon enough."

They argued over the price for a little longer, and settled on two hundred. "I'll have him fetched this afternoon," the courtier said. He and his servant left, the servant still sweating and looking thoroughly discomfited.

"Well, now," Madis said, leaning on the gatepost. "I'm fairly sure

I *didn't* just see you sell a beautiful but touchy beast to Lord Galzas."

"Some men only want a creature they can break," Dagri said. "If he had been sweet as milk, that *tsikshala* would never have bought him. But Shaikan and however many horses he decides to bring with him will be back tonight. By tomorrow, any horses that look like them will be nowhere in the city. And a certain fool will have perhaps a broken rib, or a crushed foot, and will not be riding for some time. Tea?"

"What sort of tea?"

"Weak stupid tea for weak city people," Dagri said. "For you, at least."

"Then lead on."

The house attached to the stable was small and warm. It smelled of strong herbs and baking and contained a beaming young woman very like Dagri, an equally beaming young man, and a number of brightly-dressed children who ran in and out so quickly that Madis lost count.

Dagri gestured Madis to a seat at the kitchen table. Tea appeared – weak city stuff for Madis and a concoction the colour and texture of hot, greasy mud for Dagri.

"How many people, how much loot?" Dagri said.

"People? Five at most. As to loot – one small important piece."

"All right. My sister and her husband can run the stables for a few days. One thing."

"Yes?"

"If that *tsikshala*, who dishonours the name of brother to you, should happen to harm any of my horses, I will kill him. Or Shaikan will. Or we will do it together."

"Trust me, he won't."

"I am only telling you what will happen."

"Understood."

The tiny shop was crammed between a perfumier whose average product cost more per ounce than a labourer's yearly wage and a bootmaker who clad only the most well-heeled feet in the city. Madis had dressed for the occasion; a little paint around the nose, the faint shadow of stubble and she made a perfectly unobtrusive young man, in the discreet but well-made uniform of an upper servant.

She pushed open the door on a glimmering, shifting cave of chimes and ticks and whispers. A small brass bird perched on a silver twig tilted its head and chirped at her, lifting delicately enamelled wings in shimmering blues and greens. A clock held in the arms of a pair of charming bronze dragon-nymphs declared the half-hour with a puff of scented steam that mingled with the scents of oil, brass, and extremely potent perfume suffusing the shop's interior.

Madis made her way carefully between the crammed shelves, elbows clamped to her sides. "Momenté, momenté," a voice called from somewhere in the gleaming depths. A man popped out from behind a stand of over-elaborate clocks, rubbing his hands and bowing, dressed very much like Madis except for his fat silk cravat and the ornate jeweller's glass swinging from a chain about his neck.

He took in Madis at a glance, and his deferential demeanour, along with much of his Ankarian accent, dropped away. He did his best to look down his nose at her, despite being noticeably the shorter. "Yes?"

"I'm here to see Orrie. Orivine Prett?"

The shopkeeper sniffed. "Orivine? She's *working*, if you can call it that. And I don't permit *dalliance.*"

"A family matter," Madis said. She leaned down and cupped a hand beside her mouth. "Inheritance," she whispered. "Unexpected, and *substantial*, I understand."

"Really?" The shopkeeper cleared his throat. "Orivine, Orrie, my dear, you have a visitor! *Do* go through, it's that door on the right. And ask *dear* Orrie if there's anything she needs."

The room Madis entered was brightly lit and far less cluttered than the shop, organised with an efficiency that verged on the brutal. Tools lay in gleaming rows, boxes of tiny cogs and accoutrements were lined up by size and shape, and in the middle of it a small figure with short, light brown curls, dressed in a snuff-coloured tunic with a leather apron, sat hunched on a stool, raising her head and adjusting a pair of wire-framed spectacles with extremely thick lenses. *"Dear* Orrie?" She said. "Who are you, and whatever did you say to Monsieur Pettigis?"

"He's no more a Monsieur than I am," Madis said. "I believe his sudden surge of affection was due to a rumour you're about to receive a substantial inheritance."

"Any inheritance from my lot would probably be a broken wagon and a debt to the miller." Orrie took off her spectacles again and screwed a jeweller's loupe into her eye. "Give me a moment."

Madis could make nothing of the scatter of parts on the table. She wandered back to the door and watched Monsieur Pettigis bow himself into knots in an attempt to charm a sale out of a high-nosed dowager in a jewelled hood.

"Why is your boss pretending to be Ankarian?" she said.

"Ankarian work is supposed to be the best," Orrie said. "True, some of it's pretty good, but it's not the best."

"Whose is?"

"Falsin gold-handed. Glory of the Court of Mair. Arbian of Tessery – who's an Adept as well, of course, which some might consider cheating. Other than that, the dead."

"How did you get on with your Whirligigs?"

"Oh, they're done."

"Really? What are you going to do with them?"

Orrie shrugged. "I can't sell them here, not while I'm apprenticed to Pettigis. The Guild would destroy me – and he'd help."

"It's stupid, you being apprenticed to him. You're twice the artisan he is. Ten times."

"True," Orrie took the jeweller's loupe out of her eye. "Doesn't matter. Until I've completed an apprenticeship I can't sell my own work. At least the Artisans' Guild allows women – at a price. So I make and mend for Pettigis."

"Is there anything you can't fix?"

"People."

"Ah." Madis picked up a delicate jointed brass figurine holding a flute, turning it over in her hands. "How is Enlarius?"

"Blind, crippled and robbed. How do you think he is?" Enlarius was Orrie's mentor. The Duke of Cantilia had been so pleased with the mechanical orchestra he had commissioned from Enlarius that he had, in the tradition of tyrants, had him crippled and blinded so he could not make something better for another lord. It was only through Orrie's intervention that he had made it home, and wasn't begging on the street.

Orrie sighed. "Arbian created artificial hands that *worked*, for Lord Prindis. Guided by the wearer's mind like hands of flesh. I saw them once. But they need an Adept artisan and I'm not. If I could get Enlarius to Tessery, if I could persuade Arbian to see him – I just need to harness some flying pigs to a chariot full of gold, and we'll be well away. It won't give him back his eyes, but it would be a start."

"There's a job. It won't be a chariot full of gold, but it'll be a fair chunk. No flying pigs, though."

"How much?"

"Not sure yet, but at least two thousand nobles each. More if I can swing it. And there might be a role for your Whirligigs."

Orrie looked up. "Really?"

"Be nice to see them *used*, wouldn't it? After the time you put into them?"

"Hmm."

Orrie put her tools carefully away in a soft leather roll, tied its ribbons and tucked it into a battered leather satchel. Then she slipped off her stool. "Where are we meeting?"

"The Convent of the Pure Waters. I hired a room."

"The Convent?"

"It's clean, it's quiet, and it's not where anyone would expect a meeting of thieves. Not secular ones, anyway."

As the sun sank and the light turned purple, lanterns and glows marked the market that wove along the main street of Brisha town on every third Godsday. At this time of year, the crowds didn't begin until the thick heat of the afternoon had drawn off and the sharp sudden chill of the evening had begun.

"Herbal potions! Fine herbal potions here!" The little stall – no more than a tiny hinged table and a few strips of bright cloth – displayed bottles and boxes and packets, some plainly wrapped, some brilliantly. Alina wore tatterdemalion finery in black and scarlet. Tiny bells woven into her crow-coloured curls jingled and chimed with every movement. "Perfumes sweet from distant lands, for neck and nape and hair and hands! Potions for the itch, the ache and the ague! Potions to rid you of whatever'll plague you!"

A small crowd gathered. A young girl with her mother's black curls perched on a stool behind the stall, watching solemn-eyed, clutching a stitch-faced doll.

"You, sir," Alina grinned at an ancient man leaning on a cane. "Something to help you entertain all those young ladies?"

The old man snorted and grinned, exposing one brown and crooked tooth. "Away with yer!"

"Maybe something for that old wound, eh? Ah, I know a soldier when I see one. Here." She held out a small package.

"What is it?"

"It'll help with that knee. Take a small spoonful in hot water, twice a day."

He looked down, his mouth trembling. "I can't..."

"No charge for a brave man, soldier. Your God's blessings on you." She folded his fingers over the package. "Now, you, madam. How about something for that fine young'un, whose teeth are coming through, eh? Let you both get a bit of sleep?"

Alina had an uncanny ability to spot what was wrong with each customer. Even those who had only stopped out of curiosity found themselves adeptly analysed by those bright black eyes. And for all her patter, she was, when necessary, discreet, pressing a packet into a hand and murmuring a problem and a price, sometimes before the recipient had admitted to themselves that they were in need of a cure. Most of the cures were for ailments of the body. One or two... were not.

A man of hearty physique and magnificent beard, but with shadows under his eyes and the jowly look of someone who had recently lost a deal of weight, found her hand brushing his as she murmured, "Lot of bad luck, lately, sir?"

"How..."

"Demon. Just a little'un, but nasty. I can sort that for you. Wait a moment till the crowd's thinned."

He glanced at her clothes, seeking something. "You're not..."

"No, and I don't charge their prices, neither. But you got to promise you won't peach on me."

"I won't!" he said, fervently. "It's been hanging around for weeks, wretched thing, I can't move without breaking something, my poor wife's going distracted, I dropped a vase that was the only thing she had from her mother. But Guild prices..."

She put her finger to her lips.

The crowd thinned out. When they were briefly alone, and no one was looking in their direction, she beckoned him close, frowned, and jabbed out at his shoulder. Something like a curl of black smoke coalesced there for a moment. There was an outraged chittering just on the edge of hearing, and a brief stench that had nearby stallholders looking around accusingly and waving their hands in front of their noses.

"Gone," she said. "Three nobles, if you please."

"You're a gift from the Sky God, you are," the man said. "Take four." He thrust the coins into her hand and walked off, his shoulders straighter than they had been.

The crowd gradually collected again. More coins rattled into her purse, until the small girl tugged at her skirts. "Ma." She pointed down the street, where a wink of brass gleamed among the crowd.

"Bollocks," Alina muttered. "Nib..."

"Yes, Ma."

The little girl gave a yawn so wide it seemed likely to unhinge her jaw, and said, in a much louder voice, "Ma, I'm tired."

"Oh, sweetie. All right. Sorry, everyone, got to pack up. I was enjoying meself so much with you fine folks I forgot it was past this 'un's bedtime. She's off to the convent school tomorrow!"

Murmurs of admiration and nods of approval greeted this revelation, which was, as it happened, actually true – which might have been why Nib was packing away bottles with a certain sullen emphasis.

"You study well, young'un," a matronly woman said, "and listen to the nuns. That's the way to get into a good respectable post, eh! You might end up as a lady's maid to one of the nobility!"

What Nib thought of this possible future remained unspoken, but she gave the woman a bright smile.

Another woman, her bodice dusted with flour, leaned over and pressed a coin into Nib's hand. "You buy yourself some food with that. I know them nuns. All prayer and no pastry!"

"You're very kind," Alina said, already whisking down the bright cloths, and whipping one over her head, hiding and muffling the bells. She folded the little table down to a square no bigger than a large handkerchief, which she jammed into a vast cloth bag and hoisted onto her shoulders with the rest of the gear. Nib folded up her stool, slung it over her arm, and took her mother's hand.

The two of them disappeared into the dispersing crowd just as the Guild Inspector reached the edge of it.

"I don't want to go," Nib said. "I'm *not* going to be a lady's maid. Some woman ordering me about, it'd be like the nuns *forever*."

"Is that what's bothering you? No one said you had to be a lady's maid."

"That woman at the market did."

Alina lifted her daughter onto her lap. "She doesn't know anything."

Nib poked out her lower lip and tugged at a button on her mother's dress, as though she were four, instead of nearly ten.

"Sweetheart, listen to me." Alina put a finger under her daughter's chin, tilting her head up. Oh, those eyes – the same deep green her father's had been. His eyes had been half the reason she fell for him. "You need your letters and your numbers. Even sewing's useful. You need skills you can turn to a trade, skills I can't teach you."

"I can do what you do!"

"I can teach you potions and herbs, but herbalists are common as dung. "

"And if I'm Adept?"

"You can't use it. You *know* that."

"*You* do."

"Just because I've spent my life dodging the Guild doesn't mean I want that for you. Now put that pouty lip away before a bird lands on it, wash your face, and get on."

Nib had finally slouched off, kicking at stones, when there was a knocking below. Alina edged up to the window. She had chosen this room carefully for a good view of the front door.

"Madis?"

Madis swept a bow.

"Wait there."

"Where else am I going to go?"

Alina hurtled down the stairs, flung the door open and threw her arms around Madis. "Where the hells have you been?"

"It's been less than a moon, you daft creature. It's good to see you."

"Come up, but quiet, the landlady's got ears on her like a bat."

The room was small but colourful, clothes and jewellery and trinkets draping every surface in a disorder that somehow managed to look intentional, like the interior of a fancy jewellery box. It smelled of sweet herbs and perfumes. Among the glorious frippery were a basin, a chest and a chair. Madis seated herself on the chest. "How's Nib?"

"Having her numbers hammered into her head. Poor scrap."

"What?"

"I got her into the little school the Nuns run."

"Not the Pure Waters."

"That's the one. Why?" Alina leaned forward, her face suddenly grim. "Have you heard something? Something bad?"

"No, not at all. I'm having a meeting there, that's all."

"Oh!" Alina snorted laughter.

"It's no funnier than that your daughter's being schooled there," Madis said. "Why *is* she being schooled there?"

"Because she needs skills. Specially if something happens to me. Also..." Alina sighed. "*If* something happens to me, I've contracted with the nuns to take care of her until she reaches her majority. It's a thing they do."

"Oh."

"You don't approve?"

"I just thought you'd have asked me, that's all. You know I'd take her."

"And if you're in prison? Or your head's no longer attached to your neck?"

"Well, there is that."

"So," Alina said, "What's the job, and who else is in? Oh, and has your donkey's arse of a brother fallen down a dry well yet? Please tell me he has."

The room at the convent smelled of cotton scrubbed with harsh soap and the incense that drifted from the shrine. There was a narrow bed on which Dagri and Milandree sat discussing horses as Milandree mended a strap. There were two chairs which looked so rigidly unwelcoming that Orrie had chosen instead to sit on Madis' ancient travelling chest, which was a great deal stronger and less cheap than it looked.

Alina and Madis entered together. Dagri and Milandree looked up and nodded. Orrie bounced to her feet.

Alina whisked her into a hug and let go abruptly. "Ow! You're spiky!"

"Sorry." Orrie said. "Tools." She straightened her spectacles, knocked askew by Alina's enthusiasm.

"And how's," Alina made an extravagant bow, "the most elegant Pettigis?"

Orrie rolled her eyes. "So worn out with all the bowing and scraping he hardly has the strength to take all the credit."

Alina snorted.

"Oh, here," Orrie said, digging in one of her many pockets. "This is for Nib." She held out a shiny metal figure about six inches high. It had a head and arms and torso, and a cone-shaped lower half. In one hand was a fan, and a small key was attached to its wrist on a fine chain. "Wind it up at the back, and it'll dance and open and close its fan."

"Thank you!" Alina held the little figure up to the light. "She'll love it."

"That's like one of your Whirligigs, isn't it?" Madis said.

"I made this first, to test the basic principles." Orrie said. "They're a bit more sophisticated."

"They're uncanny," Madis said.

"I thought you liked them!" Orrie's hurt expression, magnified by her spectacles, made her look like an orphaned kitten.

"That's *exactly* why I like them," Madis said, grinning.

"When will you send Nib to me, so I can teach her to ride?" Dagri said.

"Not on that terrifying beast outside, I hope." Alina peered through the window. "I didn't know horses got that big. Is he yours?"

Dagri shrugged. "He owns himself."

"Like you." Alina flung herself onto the bed, pouting. "I hope this job's a good one, Madis, I'm sick of scraping for every penny because the fucking Adepts' Guild won't let me join. Oh, unless I can come up with six thousand gold, that is."

"Six *thousand?*" Madis yelped. "I thought guild fee was two?"

"Oh, no," Alina said. "Even if they did decide to let a mere female join, you see, it would be so terribly disruptive that only an extra four thousand could even begin to compensate them for the trouble. And I'd still only ever have journeyman status, I'd never become a full Guild member."

"Six thousand, to get *journeyman* status?" Orrie frowned. "That's ridiculous. The Artisans will charge me four, but at least I end up a full Master."

"I know. But unless I can get to journeyman I haven't a hope of persuading them to let me take full status."

"Luck with that," Milandree said.

"Got to try, haven't I? If Nib turns out Adept I want her to have a chance at Guild membership, *proper* Guild membership, and it's a lot easier if you've a relative already in. Anyway never mind that. Isn't this nice? All back together! So? What's the job?"

"Have you heard that Lord Baridine has found himself a wife?" Madis said. She told them about the belt, and watched their eyes begin to gleam.

"So who's the bride?" Alina said.

"Lady Casillienne of Darnor."

Alina sat up, the bells in her hair jingling. "Darnor? *Darnor?* But that's..."

"A long way north," Madis said.

"It's not just a long way north!" Alina said. "It's a long way *ahead.* Women can join all the guilds there! Lady Casillienne's mother began it, she's Adept herself. I thought of moving there, but it's so far, and those winters... Why would someone from Darnor marry into the Baridines?"

"Seems like it was a bit of a whirlwind romance," Madis said. "Lady Casillienne was travelling near Quat Bay just before the passes closed for the winter, got separated from her entourage, her carriage broke a wheel, Lord Baridine was riding past, offered her the hospitality of his house. She went to stay and... proposal, acceptance, wedding plans. So eager she's not even waiting for the passes to open so her family can attend."

Alina scowled. "Baridine must have the charm of an incubus."

Orrie said, "Any idea where the belt was made? Or who by?"

Madis shook her head. "Not yet."

"It will help."

"I have the counterspell, but not the maker," Madis said.

"The spell might tell me something," Alina said. "And I've got a clerk friend at the Guild. There might be something in the Guild records. Magical foci are a big deal, and dangerous. Anything like that would be on record, unless it was done outside the Guild. If it was that means a very powerful maker working outside Guild law. Which is... interesting."

"Good, see what you can get," Madis said. She passed Alina a folded paper. "This is a copy of the spell. Orrie, there'll likely be a lock on Lady Casillienne's door, but the main one will be the belt."

"Are the Baridines Sky God worshipers?" Alina said. "I can deal with little air demons, but I like to know what I'm up against. Remember those toothy things guarding that strongroom in Atriani? I didn't even know there was a Weasel God until then." Alina scowled. "I didn't enjoy finding out, either. Those boots were never the same."

"Well," Madis said, "the Baridines are Sky God at least as far back as the Glass Wars – but then, if you're fighting under the banner of our beloved monarch, it would be unwise to admit to anything else. Before that, the Goddess of the Bay – Ilianu, I think. Something like that. From what I've found out so far, some of the servants probably still worship her – I would, too, if I lived on a rock in the middle of her territory."

Alina nodded. "All right, I'll prepare for both. So, how are we getting off this rock?"

"We still need to work that out."

Milandree took out one of her knives and began to sharpen it, with quick, practiced strokes. "Not going in without a full plan. Not after last time."

"Trust me," Madis said.

"You, yes. Your brother?" Milandree gave her a look as pointed as the blade.

"All right, all right!" Madis waved her hands. "I'll keep him away from us, I promise. Milandree, I need you in the palace guard."

Milandree groaned. "Socks."

"Yeah, socks. Sorry."

Orrie blinked. "Socks?"

Milandree gestured at her crotch. "Socks."

"But what for?" Orrie said.

"Bulging," Alina said. "You know. You *do* know, do you?"

"Oh! To look like... Oh."

"Orrie, darling, you need to get out more," Alina said.

Orrie was frowning at Milandree's lap.

"Oh, watch it, she's getting that look," Alina said. "I don't think Milandree wants a mechanical knob, dear." She paused. "On the other hand, I bet I could sell those..."

"Don't tell the nuns," Milandree said.

"I'm sure otherwise they'd be *totally* happy with a bunch of crooks planning a robbery in one of their rooms," Madis said.

"And how am I to join the palace guard?" Milandree said.

"I've been digging. Once the Baridine's grants from the crown proved less profitable than they hoped, the reputation they made during the siege was pretty much their only source of credit. They tend to be sentimental about it. So you, my dear, are going to be the grandson of one of the men who was in the siege. He retired over to Green Valley way, after he got injured in the war, took a wife, set up a farm, and died a couple of years back." Madis dug a sheaf of papers out of her capacious bag and thrust them at Milandree. "This is everything you need to know about your grandpa, and his part in the siege, and any other bits I could dig up."

Milandree took the papers with a sigh. "And there will be a place going in the guard?"

"Fortunately," Madis said, "one of them is an Avigani. I've arranged for a message calling him home to defend his family's honour by taking part in the latest feud with their neighbours."

"And who will you be?" Orrie asked.

"I managed to get hold of a guest list, such as it is," Madis said. "No one from Darnor, of course, so at least I don't have to try and get *that* bloody accent right. Lady Tanisal of fading but influential local gentry has been invited, presumably purely for the look of the thing, since the poor dear hasn't attended a social occasion outside her own estates in the fifteen years since her husband died. She will startle and delight them all by turning up, if they remember who she is. I've even managed to get a picture of her, though it's twenty years old and I suspect was pretty flattering at the time."

"And how do you know she won't turn up?" Alina said.

"Because she's currently confined with a badly broken ankle and won't be travelling anywhere for a while."

"Won't she have sent an apology?"

"She changed her mind, obviously, as is the gentry's privilege. Alina, you're my maid."

Alina rolled her eyes. "You think socks are bad? Yes ma'am, no ma'am, let me fasten your corset, ma'am..."

"Listen, if you can think of a better way in than as my maid, feel free," Madis said. "I've got you a background, too... Been with the family for years, you have." She smirked at Alina. "Loyal as a dog but not very bright."

"Oh, thanks."

"Dagri, we need good, fast horses. And I have plans for Shaikan, too."

"What about getting across the actual *sea*, though?" Alina said. "The bloody place is an island. Even assuming we get in all right, how the hells do we get *out*? Dagri can get the fastest horses you like, but unless they can swim... and it's a big bay. Also, archers."

"There'll be boats," Madis said. "People have to get to the island somehow."

"Madis," Alina said, "we're talking about the *only* place undefeated in the Glass Wars. Because it sits in the middle of the fucking sea. Once the guests are in it's going to be closed tight as a lockup, and the second they realise the belt is missing, they're not going to let anyone leave. What are you planning to do then? 'Oh, sorry sir, just happened to find this belt lying about, wondered who it belonged to...'"

"True," Madis said. "Until the wedding's over, there's no excuse for *anything* to leave the island... except... What do you really *not* want around during your festivities?"

"My uncle Fandik," Orrie said.

"Who?"

"A drunk. Re-fights old wars and tries to dance with people who don't want to be danced with."

"Unfortunately," Madis said, "all they're likely to do with drunken guests is get their servants to haul them to their rooms, not chuck them off the island. What else?"

"Sick people," Dagri said. "You get one sick horse in a herd, you take it away before all the others get sick."

"Wouldn't they just shove 'em in a different part of the castle?" Milandree said.

"Tricky if it's full to the brim with guests, and servants..." Madis frowned.

"The dead," Alina said. "Bad luck to have a corpse at a wedding."

Dagri raised her eyebrows. "My grandmother had a place of honour at my sister's wedding in her best robe and headdress, and she's been dead for twenty years."

"What? How?" Alina said.

"It's called taxidermy."

There was a silence that was approximately three parts fascination to two parts horror.

Madis shook her head, blinking. "Right, now I've got an image for my nightmares forever, and thank you *so* much for that, Dagri... Listen. If we can arrange for a corpse, we've got a way to get the belt off the island. Oh, don't look at me like that. You know I don't mean killing anyone."

"They'll inspect the boat," Alina said. "Or they will if they've any sense."

"So we use the corpse itself," Madis said.

Milandree snorted. "So we're going to get someone who *isn't* dead, put the belt in them, and float them away?"

"Hang on. Dagri... You just said. About your grandmother. Can you... can someone provide us with a corpse? That's hollow? And looks like a typical Quat Region noblewoman in her fifties?"

Dagri scowled. "The preservation is done to highly honoured members of the tribe, not just anyone. It takes weeks. It costs gold."

"Find out if someone will do it, in time. People die in the city every day. With a corpse and the right makeup, we can make them look like whoever we want."

Dagri shrugged. "I'll try. Can't promise."

"Good enough."

"That seems... over-elaborate?" Alina said. "There's got to be easier ways to get the belt out of there."

"I have my reasons," Madis said.

"And how do we get a corpse *in?*" Alina said.

"Rich ladies attending parties have a *great deal* of luggage," Madis said.

"Oh, yuk. And guess who'll be hauling it."

"A prepared corpse is lighter than an ordinary one," Dagri said.

Alina made a face. "That makes me feel *so* much better. So. The belt, once we've got it, is easy enough, but it'll have to be out of there fast – unless we can get it off her Ladyship and away before she notices it's gone."

"All right," Madis' face was alight. "Lady Tanisal, that is, me, gets sick with something massively infectious. Thunder plague – that'll do – and alas, dies. Her corpse, accompanied by her maid, is shipped off the island, with all the haste that can be managed – accompanied by Milandree."

"And why would they let me go?" Milandree said.

"You will have a dalliance with Lady Tanisal, and will thus be undoubtedly infected with the Thunder Plague. They'll practically shove you onto the boat."

"That gets us off the island," Alina said. "What about you, running around all alive?"

"I'll work it out," Madis waved a hand.

"Fine. And Orrie? How do we get *her* in and out?"

"That's easy." Madis grinned at Orrie. "Lady Tanisal is going to order a wedding present from Monsieur Pettigis. Designed by you, and accompanied by you. You can show the happy couple how they work. Until they don't."

"The Whirligigs. You want them to go wrong?"

"I want them to *distract*. To keep as many as possible of the guests – and the guards – occupied far from the bride's chamber and the family chapel. There's a few other details I want to discuss with you later."

"One thing we have not mentioned." Dagri said. "What is the *tsikshala's* part in this?"

"What *does* that word mean?" Alina propped her chin on her hand. "I've been wanting to ask."

"It means what Orrie wants to make and you want to sell. A prick, without a brain or a heart."

"A more perfect description of your brother I never heard," Alina said. "So, Madis darling, what aren't you telling us?"

"All right," Madis said. "My brother is the one the buyer approached. He wants us to do the job, and he'll take half."

"Half?" Alina squeaked.

Dagri let out a stream of words which needed little translation.

Orrie rolled her eyes.

Milandree sighed, and put the knife away.

"Wait!" Madis said. "All of you, please. I have some thoughts." She grinned like a shark. "You'll like them, I promise."

"Orivine! Orivine!" The carefully-modulated voice Pettigis used for his customers had risen to a rusty creak.

"Yes?"

"Stop what you're doing and come here!"

Orrie, with some relief, ceased fiddling with the mainspring of a clock of such grandiose ugliness that it achieved a form of magnificence, if not actual beauty. It had been ordered for the Duke of Bendarish and would almost certainly never be paid for.

"What is it?" She emerged to find Pettigis pink-faced and wide-eyed, waving a piece of paper.

"We have an order! A wonderful order! But we can't do it! It's impossible!"

"What is it?"

"We are to provide a gift for Lord Baridine's wedding. But it's in less than a moon!" He began to flitter around the shop, picking things up, staring at them, and thrusting them back onto their shelves. "No,

37

no... we have nothing, nothing suitable. Why are you just standing there? This could make my name, don't you understand? Lord Baridine's wedding to Lady Casillienne of Darnor! It has to be *magnificent!*"

"What are the chances of our actually getting paid, this time?"

"Oh, really, you have such a *mercenary* mind. This will be a gift for one of the oldest families in the *land.* Lady Casillienne is, well, Northern, of course, and a reputation for being very *modern...* but I'm sure he'll tame her eccentricities. And in any case... Oh, it has to be *exceptional.* A clock? No, no, what nonsense, something truly... that mechanical swan that Brevatish made for Lord Modicar's wedding, now that was... but two years in the making... It can't be done!"

Orrie allowed him to ramble, occasionally dropping in a suggestion that might almost have been calculated to increase his panic. "There was a cage of mechanical birds for the Prevani wedding. But that took *four* years, I understand."

"Four!" His voice rose to a shriek. "And are you suggesting I should *imitate* another *artist?*"

She refrained from pointing out that he had been considering just that... and had, indeed, done it on numerous occasions, not only imitating but frankly stealing. Mainly, recently, from her.

"I do have something I've been working on," she said. "In my spare time."

"Oh, really? Some crude mechanism, some piece of girlish folly? You do *realise* the importance of this, do you?"

Orrie shrugged. "Given that the time is so short... but that's the gentry for you. They don't understand that an artist like yourself needs time to work."

She could feel her eyes trying their best to roll like marbles on a slope, but Madis had suggested the wording, and indeed, Pettigis was nodding solemnly. "Well, well, the gentry have other responsibilities, you know. Show me what you have, perhaps if it's not too crude, something can be made of it."

Pettigis spent so little time in the workshop that he had never noticed the cloth-draped forms in the corner.

Orrie, with a slight theatrical flair she realised, with quiet internal amusement that she had picked up from Madis, whisked the cloth away.

The Whirligigs stood side by side. From the waist up, they were roughly human, from the waist down, each was the shape of an elongated bell. They stood at the height of an average full-grown man. Their faces were stylised masks, with high cheekbones, flying brows, and full lips. Their eyes were large, catlike ovals of bright green glass, backed with mirrors to make them gleam. The 'female' torso – the one she called Spin – hinted at the curve of breasts, the mask slightly rounder in its curves – the 'male' – Reel – a little wider in the shoulders, a little squarer in the jawline. They spoke as much to the expectations of the viewer as to any inherent quality. Once they were clothed, of course, these suggestions would be heightened.

Pettigis regarded them for a moment in silence, his eyes crawling jealously over their elegant lines. "I see," he said. "And do they *do* anything?"

Instead of answering, Orrie went behind them. There were some clicks and clangs, and a tinkling, silvery music began to play.

The Whirligigs turned to each other, and bowed.

Reel held out his sleekly jointed hands.

Spin put one hand upon his 'waist' and one upon his shoulder.

With a strange, careful grace, they began to dance, sliding around each other, turning in a slow circle. Their bell-like lower bodies somehow gave the impression that feet moved swiftly below them.

As the music ran down, they slowed, bowed, parted, and returned to their standing position.

Pettigis, who had been watching with his mouth agape, rapidly pulled himself together. "Hmm," he said. "Well, I suppose one could do something with these. Possibly."

He walked around the Whirligigs. One of them let out a low 'pung' when he passed, and Orrie pretended not to notice him jump. He opened the back panel of Spin and peered at the wheels, arms and levers inside, going, "Hah," and "Hmm," and "I see." He made as though to poke the mechanism with one extremely clean and well-manicured finger, appeared to think better of it, and shut the door.

"They would require clothing appropriate to the Court." He glanced at Orrie, in her battered and practical garments. "I suppose I had better deal with *that* part of it, as well."

Orrie did not ask him 'As well as what?'. She already knew that the rest of his contribution would involve fussing, shouting, and taking the credit.

She allowed herself a small and private smile.

They met again at the Black Pig, in Madis' room.

"This is impossible," Alina complained, cramped and wriggling on the bed between Milandree and Orrie. "Have you actually *had* any company while you've been staying here? They can't have been very big... and where are you keeping your clothes?"

"Oh, stop moaning, and stay *still*," Orrie said. "This is bad enough without you scriggling about like a two-year-old."

The window of Madis' room was open a fraction, letting in the reek of beer, horses, sewage, a sudden savoury waft of hot meat pies, the rattle of passing vehicles and clatter of feet, and an occasional expression of admiration at the sight of Shaikan, tied up outside.

"So," Madis said. "Alina?"

"I've set wards."

Madis glanced at Dagri, who nodded. She went on: "Just to go over it finally, so everyone's on board. Alina and I will embark with most of the other wedding guests, two nights before the wedding. Milandree – you've applied for the guard, yes?"

"Yes. Been accepted pending proving myself capable. Going over in a few days."

"Alina? The belt?"

"Haven't found a bloody thing. Either it wasn't made under Adepts' Guild regulations or it wasn't listed as a focus. The unlocking spell isn't helping – it's very old-fashioned, could be from any of half a dozen schools." She scowled. "It's odd, for an unlocking spell, too. Really strong, which means the *locking* spell was really strong. This belt's powerful. Once we've got it we need it off our hands as soon as possible. If the Guild catches us with something with that much punch, *especially* if it's unregulated..." She shuddered.

"It'll be off our hands that night," Madis said. "Orrie, how badly do you need to know what sort of lock it is?"

Orrie frowned at the ceiling, absently shifting to try and give herself more room. "You're sure it has to be unlocked, not broken off?"

Madis made a face. "The buyer was apparently very firm on that point. If it's broken, it will stop working and be worthless to them."

Orrie sighed. "I can probably do it, if it isn't something completely mad, and you can get me enough time."

In the street, Shaikan stamped and nickered.

"So," Milandree went on, after a moment. "There'll be a big feast, followed by a display of the wedding gifts. The bride, traditionally, leaves early to get a good night's sleep before the wedding and the rigours of the wedding night. Which is good for us, but how early is up to her and the custom of the house. From what I've found out about the Baridines, they tend to run it late – but the wedding ceremony itself is set for early the following day – just after dawn."

"Just after *dawn?*" Alina groaned. "That's uncivilised."

"Too right," Madis said. "And it means we have to make sure everything is *thoroughly* sorted before that. How're the Whirligigs, Orrie?"

"They'll make my boss's name," Orrie said, with a small and slightly disconcerting smile.

"Wonderful. That and the early night should give us time before everyone else returns from the feast. So. She'll have at least one maid, and we have to assume at least one guard on the door. Milandree, if you can get posted to the door, that'll save time."

"See what I can do."

"Anyway I trust you to deal with any guards. Get in, get the belt – then there's the exciting part, getting away."

"Because the rest of it will be as calm as a bowl of soup by the fire," Alina said.

"I have faith in you all," Milandree said. "So. I get sick and am isolated from the other guests. The night before the wedding my 'corpse' goes out in the boat, accompanied by a young guard," she pointed at Milandree, "who had the misfortune to dally with the sick woman the night before, and is already showing signs of fever. Dagri? Do we have a corpse?"

"I found someone," Dagri said. "It will be fifty gold, I must make a generous offering at the shrine of his ancestors and he will only do it because he is already in disgrace."

"Fifty gold?" Milandree grumbled. "Could get a decent sword for that."

"Alina, Milandree and the corpse land at the market quay on Quat bay, probably... what, around dawn? There's an abandoned shepherd's hut just up the sheep track behind the quay – wait for us there. Dagri will collect you and bring you back here. Then we'll meet up with Arden. And if he doesn't have our share of the money already in hand, he doesn't get the belt."

"Bloody right," Milandree said.

"As soon as it's discovered the belt's missing," Madis said, "there will no doubt be a huge hue and cry and everyone will be searched. Also, they'll certainly send someone after the boat. Dagri, you'll need to get out of there fast."

"That will not be a problem."

"I don't like leaving you all behind," Alina said.

Madis smiled at her. "It won't be for long. Now, even if they do realise the belt's already gone, we can't assume that they won't search everyone after the wedding. Once all that's over, I will insinuate myself into the entourage of one of the wedding guests, and get off the island when they all leave, along with Orrie and her boss, and will then meet up with you all back here. Everyone clear?"

"I still don't trust your brother," Alina said.

"No one trusts your brother," Dagri said.

"He wants me on his team," Madis said. "If he plays us false, he won't get me."

A figure in the blue and white robes of a Priest of the Sky God, head reverently bowed, moved away from the window. It walked slowly down the street until it was out of sight of the inn, pushed back its hood, and grinned. "Oh, little sister," Arden said. "You and your friends are almost clever."

Orrie frowned up at Shaikan as the group left the Black Pig some time later. "Are you *sure* he'll do all that?" she said. "I mean, he's a *horse.*" Shaikan gave her a look. "Well I'm sorry," she said, "but you are. A very beautiful horse, but still."

"He's proved pretty useful already," Alina pointed out.

Dagri only smiled.

A day later, Madis walked into an inn called the Jug of Ale to see her brother in a particularly flamboyant jacket of green velvet with large gold buttons. A matching hat lay on the table.

"My dear... brother," Arden said. "How very plain you look."

"Thank you." Madis, dressed as a young man of moderate but respectable means, bowed. "I see *you're* not worried about attracting attention."

Arden flicked a lacy cuff. "I can avoid attention if I so wish, my dear, I simply don't see the need. After all, look at them." He waved at the roomful of traders, farmers, drapers and shopkeepers. "Dull as a November day. Obsessed with cattle and grain and cloth. Hardly a risk."

"If you find the inn so dull, why did you choose it?"

"I didn't want you to feel out of place. So what did you want to discuss?"

"We need more information on the belt."

"You have the spell, what else do you need?"

"The *make*, Arden. The make. There are thousands of different types of lock in the world. Without knowing the make the chances of getting it off without damaging it, or for that matter waking its wearer..."

Arden tutted. "I thought that Artificer of yours was supposed to be good."

"She is good. But this is not exactly the simplest job. I'm not going ahead without that information, it's too much risk. As it is the others think I'm a fool to trust you after last time."

"So like women to exaggerate. You all survived, didn't you?"

"Barely. Get me that information, by tonight, or we're pulling out."

At that moment, the server brought their food. Arden poked at his fish with the tip of his knife and sighed. "This looks appallingly overcooked. Take it away, and tell whoever passes for a cook in this place that I'll have the duck, and to try not to make a mess of it."

The woman was not out of earshot when he added, "Honestly, if she'd looked any more like the fish I might have taken my knife to her by mistake. You'd think they could find people who wouldn't put a man off his food. Are you *eating* that?"

"It's perfectly fine," Madis said. "In fact, it's good."

"You never did have any palate."

"Can you get me that information?"

"Yes, I can get you that information; really, do you want me to hold your hand as well? I'll meet you back here, tonight. At supper hour, *not* that I plan to eat here again."

Arden left the inn, smiling to himself. He walked through the lamplit, cooling streets, occasionally pausing to comment on a shapely figure or swipe a piece of fruit from a market stall. Eventually he reached a small boarding house, so tucked away that it might have been chosen for its obscurity. It smelled of cheap stew and damp.

He was let in by a colourless fellow who, once he gathered that Arden had no intention of taking a room for the night, appeared to lose all interest in anything but returning to the meagre fire in the front room and the steaming brew beside it.

The woman who was waiting for Arden in the cold, under-furnished upstairs room was slight and pale, her gown of good cut but plain cloth. She had discreet glints of gold in her ears and on her fingers, and a hint of the North in an otherwise courtly accent.

He gave her one of his most charming smiles, which, yet again, she utterly failed to return.

"Well?"

Arden bowed. "All is going as planned. I have enlisted some assistance, but you can be assured that I will myself supervise everything."

"You understand, the belt must be removed without any harm coming to the wearer. That would damage the magic and render it useless to me. And you will not be paid."

"Indeed, you have been most clear on that point. Several times, in fact."

"Good."

"Now, I don't wish to seem ungentlemanly," Arden seated himself in one of the rickety chairs, stretching out his legs and admiring the gloss of his boots, "but I require some assurance of goodwill before we proceed further."

"I assume you mean money."

"If you must put it so crudely."

"You are a thief," she said. "How else should I put it?"

Arden's head came up, and he shot a glare of dislike at the

woman. Her pale eyes met his expressionlessly. Remembering that she was, if not herself gifted with powerful magic, certainly working for someone who was, he reined in his temper.

"You will be paid when I have the belt, and not before," she said. "There are other thieves."

"The best of them are already working for me," he said. "And as there are other thieves, so there are undoubtedly other buyers."

Those pale eyes met his again. "By all means," she said, "you may attempt to find one, in the time that remains before the wedding, who understands the true value of the belt."

Arden felt a squirm of unease. The woman was remarkably self-confident, which furthered his belief that she herself was the possessor of magical ability. And the belt she described to him – heavy, ugly, inscribed with crude symbols – would fetch nothing like the amount she was offering on the open market, but was unusual enough to be extremely easy to trace. A fast, guaranteed sale was by far the better risk.

Arden had no problem with risk – especially when it was taken by others – but he liked to have something to show for it, and to be in a state to enjoy that something.

He had no idea why it had to be obtained before the wedding. Perhaps it was something to do with virginity. He speculated briefly on the woman before him and decided that she was almost certainly a virgin, and anyone attempting to remedy that condition would probably end up with a very unfortunate case of frostbite.

A spatter of what sounded like sleet hit the window. His boots would rapidly lose their polish in this weather. The thought did nothing to relieve his irritation.

"Was there anything else?" she said.

"A little more information," he said. "The origins of the belt."

"Origins?"

"Some information about its maker, where it came from. My Artificer requires it, in order to ensure it is removed safely."

"It was bought, or traded from, Defani. That is all I have."

"Then that will have to do."

"Was that all?" The woman said.

"There remains only the arrangement of the handover," Arden

said. "Here?"

"For now. If that needs to change I will send you a message."

If he had not found her so irritating he would have admired her discretion. He had made enquiries, but had succeeded in discovering nothing whatsoever about the woman – it was as though she had simply popped into existence in this dull little room, in her dull gown.

Except for that accent, and those glints of gold, she could be an upper servant.

Sleet hit the window again, along with a piece of moss dislodged from the gutter. The weather would get no better, and he would obviously gain nothing more from her tonight. Arden stood up, and bowed. "I will take my leave of you, then, Madam. And I look forward to seeing you when I have the belt."

She gave him the barest of nods in return. Arden closed the door of the house behind him with slightly unnecessary force, and occupied his return journey with a series of pleasant meditations on the fate of women who thought too highly of themselves.

Neither he, nor the woman in the room, noticed the shadow that dropped with catlike agility from the roof of the boarding house to the street, and disappeared down an alleyway.

Three

On the afternoon before the wedding, Madis joined the rest of the guests in the great hall of Baridine Castle, where a luncheon was about to be served. The shutters were open, but the morning's sun had disappeared, and a thick coat of grey cloud was rapidly rolling in over the sea.

Most of the light came from the bluish glow of hundreds of dancing werelights and the mellow gleam of thousands of candles. It glittered on wrought silver, gleamed from polished wood, deepened the hue of rich velvets and slick satins, caught fire in the jewels at ears and throats and wrists. In this room alone was enough easily portable loot to make the fingers itch.

Guards stood at every entrance. Above each door, window and hearth, according to Alina, were wards. Madis spotted a sigil or two, black and spiky, half hidden behind the woven garlands of purple and scarlet lilies. The flowers alone, at this time of year, must have cost the price of a good riding horse. It seemed Lord Baridine was *very* sure this wedding was going to restore his fortunes.

The garlands' heavy scent mingled not quite happily with the odours of food, perfumes, beeswax polish and sweat. Those lilies could be found in hangings and carvings throughout the castle, as well as the servants' livery. The Baridines were selectively proud of their family history, especially their support for the current successful claimant to the throne, which, if history went their way, would no doubt be translated as undying loyalty to the True Line.

However poorly rewarded such loyalty was currently proving to be.

The solution to that unfortunate state of affairs, the Lady Casillienne of Darnor, was even now taking her place between Lord Baridine and his formidable mother, the Dowager Lady Baridine.

Lady Casillienne was a tall woman with the yellow hair and white-rose complexion typical of the far northerner. She was currently unflatteringly swathed in an absurd concoction that was made of enough plum-coloured silk to curtain a four-poster bed.

Madis watched the betrothed couple, her persona as nobility of the middle-to-upper sort having placed her reasonably close to the high table.

Lady Casillienne was handsome enough, but rather lacking in animation for the woman Alina had described with such enthusiasm. Baridine – in plum-coloured velvet to match the lady's silks, which flattered his more florid complexion no better than it did her pale one – had probably been good-looking enough before the drink started to blur his edges, but had an unattractive air of proprietary smugness and no obvious signs of incubus-like charm.

Yet when she could hear them over the babble, they seemed amicable enough. "Oh, yes, we're both looking forward to tomorrow!" Baridine chortled. "Eh, my dear? Can't wait, can we?" He said, looking her in the eyes.

"Can't wait," she said, though her expression remained calm.

Madis shrugged mentally. She had never attended the Darnor court; such restraint might be their style. Besides, marriage was a mystery, and among this class, little more than a trade contract as often as not. Perhaps the runaway romance was no more than a marketplace rumour. Perhaps the timing of the wedding was carefully chosen to prevent having to find accommodation for a horde of northern relatives, courtiers and hangers-on.

None of it mattered. Only the belt, somewhere under all that silk. At least, Madis *hoped* it was there.

Otherwise, all this effort was going to be of very little point.

On the other side of Baridine sat an austerely handsome young man in robes of cerulean blue and a white and grey stole. The Sky God priest, who would preside over the wedding.

That gave Madis pause. According to her researches, the Sky God priest attached to Baridine Castle was an elderly man, who had served the family since the Glass Wars. Had he died in the meantime? But she had been keeping a very careful ear for any news that came out of Brute Rock, in case it impacted their plans, and had heard nothing of such a death. Perhaps the old fellow was training a successor? There was no sign of him on the dais, but at his age, he might have cried off from a late night and a heavy meal.

Still, it troubled her that she had heard nothing of a new priest. She made a note to speak to Alina.

Luncheon was long and elaborate. Madis enjoyed every mouthful she allowed herself – too hearty an appetite might arouse suspicion – and occasionally patted her brow with a silk kerchief. She had employed paint with care, to suggest an older woman still trying to look youthful, but with a slightly-too-fervent flush to her cheeks and shadows under her eyes.

She caught sight of Milandree, on guard at one of the doors, every inch the strapping young soldier. Madis wondered how many propositions she would be turning down this evening as drink nibbled away at the guests' sense of propriety, and how Alina was getting on, down in the servants' quarters.

She hoped Orrie and Pettigis had arrived by now. She had seen no sign of them, but then, being artisans, they wouldn't be permitted to mingle with the noble guests until the gift was put on display.

The cream of the local nobility, or, at least, that substance that had floated to the top of it, were gossiping happily. Madis' lefthand neighbour, Baron Guland, a beaky fellow who had called for more wine before the second course, peered up at the dais. "Hmm. Seems fairly well behaved, for a Northerner. Thought she'd be drinking the gravy, what?" He grasped his goblet and waved it in the air. "More wine, here!" A fat ruby on his forefinger caught the light.

"She's hardly eating at all," the Baroness, on the other side, waved a fork laden with plump partridge breast and dripped sauce onto the table. "Afraid to let him see her appetite, I'll be bound. It'll all be different once she's caught him, you mark my words." She dabbed at her chin, beneath which glimmered a set of emeralds, which would have looked much better had they not also been accompanied by a double rope of pearls and several ostentatious brooches placed apparently at random about the bodice of her shocking pink gown.

"Vulgarity will out, you know."

"I've been somewhat secluded of late," Madis said. "I've heard very little of her."

The Baroness's eyes glittered with the potential for gossip. "My dear, she's a *hoyden*. Travels with hardly any servants, with whom, I hear, she's *excessively* familiar. *"* She leant close, and whispered, "rides in *breeches*. It's quite true, I had it from my cousin, who had it from someone who saw her."

The Baron snorted. "Wonder what's under 'em, eh? Bet Baridine might be in for a bit of a shock tomorrow night, eh?"

"My *Lord!"* The Baroness gasped, snickering.

"Did she not bring servants with her?" Madis said.

"You didn't hear? Got separated from them, such as they were," the Baron said. "Don't know where they disappeared off to, ran off as soon as her eye was off them, no doubt. That's what happens if you don't maintain proper distance, servants think they can get away with anything. Suppose Baridine will have provided her with some from his household."

"It doesn't look as though he troubled to provide her with someone who can dress hair," the Baroness said, peering up at the bride-to-be. "That's barely a style at all!"

"It probably is in the North," the Baron said.

"They've put her in the old West Wing," the Baroness said, smirking. "Which was last refurbished before the Glass Wars. The Lady Dowager's doing, I'll be bound. *Her* nose has been put properly out of joint."

The Lady Dowager was, indeed, looking frosty, but it was hard to imagine her looking anything else.

Madis glanced at the door, where new guards were taking the place of the old. Shift change. Madis pressed a hand to her brow. "Oh, dear, I don't feel quite... *Do* excuse me."

She made her way out of the dining room and moved through the corridors, weaving slightly and tugging the neck of her gown lower, a tipsy – or sickly – guest feeling the heat, stopping occasionally to press a hand to her stomach.

She had in fact visited the solar several times already, making sure that she was seen every time, and each time leaving looking a little greyer and walking a little more slowly.

The timing had to be right. The characteristic purplish rash of Thunder Plague could not appear too soon.

She crossed the courtyard, and stopped as a tall figure emerged. "These are the guards' quarters, madam. Permit me to escort you where you wish to go?" Milandree looked positively sinister, her eyes gleaming in the shade of her helmet.

"Oh! Oh, you startled me."

"My apologies, madam."

"I seem to have got myself quite turned about," Madis said. "The castle is so very large!"

"Indeed. Loar!"

Another guard appeared, glanced at Madis' cleavage and hurriedly away. "Mil?"

"Lady's got herself lost. Just going to... ah... escort her back to her friends."

Madis giggled and clutched at Milandree's arm. The other guard failed to conceal a smirk. "Take your time, mate, take your time."

They moved away, Madis allowing more giggles and a squeak to trail behind her as she went.

"Very nice," Milandree said as they entered Madis' room. Alina was already there, mixing up a powder.

"The fireplace smokes like a smithy and they seem to have stuffed this bed with cabbages," Madis said. "I don't think Lady Tanisal is a terribly honoured guest. Still, I'm shortly to die on this mattress, so with any luck they'll throw it out and the next person will have a better night. Either of you seen Orrie? Please tell me they've arrived."

"I saw them unloading this afternoon," Alina said. "And that will be the last boat to the island until after the wedding."

"So what have you found out?" Madis said.

"There's two guards on Lady Casillienne's bedroom at all times," Milandree said. "The room has a lock. On the outside. Seems it was kept for a relative who went a bit touched and started wandering about without his breeches. Funny thing, though... Relative died ten years back. Lock looks brand new, to me."

"Odd," Madis said.

"Very," Alina said. "And I'll tell you what else – Lady Casillienne doesn't have a maid assigned to her, it's anyone who can be spared. And no one wants to do it."

"Why not?"

"They say she doesn't even speak, stares right through them. And never gives presents. Creepy *and* mean. I don't know about you, Madis, but this is beginning to feel a little... off, to me."

Madis rubbed at her mouth. "Well, it makes our lives easier. If she doesn't have her own maid, there's no one keeping an eye on her. What about the wards?"

"I had a good look," Alina said. "Mid-level adept stuff, nothing I can't handle. It's mostly around the dining hall and her Ladyship's chamber – a *lot* around the chamber."

"Any god-related stuff?"

"Not that I've noticed. Why?"

"Because the Castle's Sky-God priest seems to have been unexpectedly replaced with a younger version. Hear anything downstairs?"

"One old biddy did mention something about the old Father being put to pasture, but like you said the house servants mostly aren't Sky God followers, so they didn't pay much attention."

"Well, keep your eyes open. Now, the guards. Milandree?"

"Got myself on the late shift," Milandree said, "but there's an extra guard. So three of us."

"You can handle two, with one hand behind your back," Milandree said.

"Maybe. But." Milandree's coppery brows drew down over her bright hazel eyes, giving her the look of an angry hawk. "No one allowed in or out. Not even a maid. Not even *her*. She tries, we're to – politely – stop her. Captain says she sleepwalks."

"Three guards to stop someone sleepwalking?"

"Yes."

"And no one allowed in? What if she needs something?"

Milandree shrugged. "She's not known for wanting much. Doesn't make demands. Hardly speaks."

Madis chewed her lip. "You're right, Alina, this is definitely beginning to sound a little odd." There was a splashing sound. "Is there a leak in here? It's started raining."

"No," Alina said, pointing at the battered dresser. "Look."

The jar with the little god in it was rocking as its occupant thrashed about inside. "I'd better top it up again," Alina said. "It seems to keep it quiet."

"You remembered to use fresh water?" Madis said.

"Of course I did. You're not telling *me* how to deal with a god, are you?"

"No, Alina, I'm not. But *have* you? Have you found out anything about it yet? Because you said..."

"What with running around being your maid, your ladyship, trying to find out more about the setup here, and practicing the release spell for the belt, I've hardly had time! You're the one who insisted on buying it, *you* find out!"

"I'm not the expert, as you just reminded me!"

"Shut it." They both turned to look at Milandree, who was glowering. "We're in enemy territory with insufficient intelligence," she said. "Which is bad enough. *Don't break the line.*"

Madis sighed. "Sorry. Sorry, Alina. My nerves are all in a twist."

"All right," Alina said. "You're right, Milandree. Look, something's bothering our little friend in the jar, but it'll have to wait. I was hoping I'd get into Her Ladyship's room ahead of time, but it looks as if you're going to have to get me in with Orrie."

"Where *is* she?" Madis said.

At that moment there was a knock. Milandree stepped behind the curtains, Alina flung a cloth over the jar and began folding petticoats.

"Who is it?" Madis called.

"Who d'you think?" Orrie growled. "Bloody let me in."

Madis leapt up and did so. "Thank the little gods, I was wondering what had happened."

Orrie was flushed and sweating, her clothes stained with oil, her spectacles smeared and her curls apparently having a competition to see how far they could stand out from her head.

"Pettigis happened, that's what. We almost missed the boat. I've spent the time since we arrived persuading him that he needs to concentrate on his appearance, and leave the actual work to me, which was *surprisingly* difficult. Also, this place is a bollocking maze and I didn't dare ask directions, because why would an artisan be looking for Lady Tanisal's room? How long have we got?"

"It'll be tight," Milandree said. "Shift change every two hours. They're twitchy."

"Let's hope Her Ladyship decides to retire before midnight," Madis said. "That gives us an hour to deal with the guards, get in, work the spell and the lock, get out, and for Alina to come and find me dead, raise the alarm and you two to get my corpse on the boat. Orrie, is your distraction all set?"

"Yes."

"Are you certain they're going to let me go?" Alina said.

"You've been nursing a Thunder Fever victim. They'll practically throw you in the sea themselves. They're almost certainly going to come after you once the alarm's raised, though, so you'd better poke it. How fast can you sail?"

"Oh please," Alina grinned. "I'm a smuggler's daughter. I've outrun the coastguard in a boat that was little more than a barrel with a sail on it. Only problem will be if it stays a flat calm, I might have to help things along a bit, and the weather gods *really* don't like that." The jar sloshed harder, and Alina jumped to her feet, grabbed the ewer on the chest of drawers, took off the lid and poured a little water in. "There. Happy now?" The water darkened as though the little god were bleeding thick black smoke, and the sloshing stilled. Alina frowned at it, put the lid back on, and sat down again.

"Right, supper's in less than two hours. Everyone ready?"

Alina entered the castle's vast kitchen and immediately prickled with sweat. Both its huge hearths and all of its ovens were aroar. In one hearth a glistening beef carcass turned slowly on the spit as a pair of kitchen brats heaved on the handles, in the other bubbled a series of cauldrons, hanging at different heights. The air was full of greasy steam smelling of baking, gravy, sweat and spilled wine. The head cook, a tall, skinny man, his hair bound in a red scarf and his deep brown skin gleaming, directed scurrying minions, using a ladle like a general's baton and swearing in at least three languages and one he might have made up.

Alina kept out of his way, and approached a grey-haired woman with impressively muscled arms who had paused after lifting a batch of sugar-cakes from the oven to gulp from a tankard of water, and leaned close as though telling a secret. "Please, ma'am, is there something here I could use for a tisane, for fever?"

"Fever?" The woman swiped at her brow with a limp rag and tucked it back in her apron pocket. She eyed Alina's upper-servant clothes and decided to be polite. "What sort of fever?"

"I'm not sure," Alina said. "It's for my mistress. She was well enough yesterday, but now she's proper sickly, been running to the solar all day and now she's taken to bed."

"There's some herbs in that cupboard over there," the baker said. "Star of the sea, in the blue jar, and dragonroot, in the wooden box with the dragon carved on the lid. Spoonful of each steeped in a cup of hot water, that'll take the fever down." She turned back to her cakes.

"Thank you." Alina gathered the herbs and took a cup of water from one of the cauldrons. On the way out, she said, "Let's hope it takes down the swelling as well. She looks like a frog, poor lady!"

"Wait. Swelling? In the neck?"

Alina pretended not to hear and whisked herself out of the kitchen.

"I've cast the net," Alina said, setting the mug on the chest. "All the gods, woman, you look terrible." She glanced at the thing on the bed. "You *both* look terrible. This is really... disturbing."

"*You* find it disturbing?" Madis grimaced. The corpse looked a great deal like her – especially since both their faces were painted to yellowish pallor, both their throats puffed with a judicious application of soft paste, and both their lips an unlovely shade of purplish blue.

"You're sure about this."

"I'm sure."

"Your brother..."

"I said, I'm sure."

"All right." Alina cocked her head. "Wind's getting up. Hope it doesn't get much worse."

"Me too. Right, they should be finishing dinner about now. Get going. I'm going to let myself be seen like this near Lady Casillienne's rooms – might help discourage anyone from hanging about – then I'll get this shit off me and get into my skivvy gear."

"Be careful."

"Always. You too."

They hugged, briefly – and carefully, so as not to dislodge any of Madis' makeup – and left the room, both determinedly not looking at the corpse on the bed.

The party, such as it was, was well under way. The guests, having dined (again), had made their way to the main hall of the castle. The current fashions being wide, frilled and furbelowed meant that the paucity of wedding guests was slightly less obvious than it might have been – but only slightly. Lord Baridine seemed to have confined his guest list to those he hoped to impress or to whom he owed money. There were no members of the royal family – the Baridines no longer wielded that kind of influence.

The absence of anyone from her court or her family seemed not to bother Lady Casillienne – but then, very little seemed to trouble her, or affect her at all. She sat, gazing over the crowd, dressed in yet another extravagant gown, (this one a deep blue that suited her a little better than the previous night's plum). Brilliants glimmered about her neck and wrists.

Her husband to be gulped at his wine, his expression flickering between triumph and nerves, his eyes darting around the crowd, glancing frequently at the ancient clock that stood on the black marble mantelpiece at the end of the hall, the sun and moon on its face parading serenely through the hours, its pendulums reflecting gleams from the candles and werelights as they swung.

Orrie had taken a thorough look at the clock earlier, and dismissed it as adequate but not exceptional.

Now, dressed inconspicuously in buff wool, she stood behind Pettigis, who was flamboyant in scarlet velvet and ribbons, as he muttered over his introduction. The Whirligigs were in wheeled wooden boxes. Orrie and one of the castle servants stood ready to wheel them into the hall, Pettigis having been too mean to hire his own servants for the purpose.

The clock chimed eleven.

"Time to put the bride to be to bed!" Baridine roared.

"But..." Pettigis sputtered. "The parade... the gifts..."

The guests too murmured, glancing at each other. Putting the bride to bed *before* the gifts were paraded was simply not done. "Overeager, isn't he?" Baron Guland said, in a voice intended to be overheard.

"Well, *really,*" sniffed the Baroness. "So *rude.*"

The Dowager leaned over and whispered something to Lord Baridine. He pouted like a sulky child, then put on a conciliatory smile. "Forgive my wife to be," he called. "She is weary, and wishes to be at her best tomorrow. She will go, and I will stay, and witness your most kind generosity!"

"Ah. *Northern* manners," said a broad-shouldered man in a green satin jerkin, so heavily embellished with gold thread it was a wonder he could support its weight.

"Well, I hope she learns how to behave," said his companion, flicking her fan so vigorously one of the many crystals sewn to it flew off and landed in someone's wine. "Very poor taste. Very poor."

Orrie took off her spectacles and cleaned them, returning them to her nose in time to see Lady Casillienne leaving the room, closely escorted by a twitchy-looking maid and two of the castle guards.

Baridine settled himself back down, called for more wine, and ordered the musicians to play.

The parade of gifts began. Some ugly silver goblets, a rather small hanging depicting the Siege (someone was currying favour but not trying very hard), a roll of silk that looked a little cracked and faded, possibly from being stored overlong. The name of each giver was announced, while Baridine tried to look pleased and smug, and succeeded mainly in looking sulkily constipated while sneaking constant glances at the clock.

Since the only other mechanism was a singing bird designed by Pettigis that had been sold from his shop over a year ago, at a discount, due to its habit of sudden, unmusical squawks, there was nothing of interest to Orrie. She focussed on wheeling forward the box, and setting it carefully upright. There was a faint, silvery chiming noise as she did so.

Pettigis swept forward and bowed deeply, his ribbons flickering. "A gift from Lady Tanisal," he announced. "In memory of her beloved husband, Lord Tanisal, who passed from us fifteen years since, in the hope that this marriage will be as happy and as long as theirs, designed by Abianus Pettigis."

Orrie mentally rolled her eyes at the implication that Abianus Pettigis had designed Lady Tanisal's marriage.

The crowd peered, intrigued.

Orrie caught the servant's eye, and they both leaned down, and opened the cases.

Inside, the Whirligigs gleamed softly. The elaborate clothes in which they had been dressed made them look not more human, but somehow less – the ruffles and lace emphasising the cold pure lines of their masks. The crowd gasped and murmured.

Orrie allowed herself a small sigh. They really were rather good.

With a faint whirr, the Whirligigs stepped out, faced each other, bowed.

Each wore a long robe, which rendered Reel a little old-fashioned, but was necessary to hide its bell-shaped lower half.

The crowd *oohed* and applauded.

The Whirligigs danced. By the time they finished, the crowd was pressing in, reaching out to touch. "Ladies, Gentlemen, please!" Pettigis cried. "The mechanisms are very delicate! Lord Baridine? Lord Baridine, these were designed for you and your lady wife. Would you do my creation the great, the *singular* honour of dancing with the lady of the pair?"

"Hah!" Baridine, his face flushed with wine and restored good humour, bounded down from the dais. "Why not? So long as I don't make that metal fellow jealous, what?"

There was a scatter of laughter at this sally, but out of Baridine's earshot, there were sharper remarks about whether he would find his metal dance-partner any colder than his bride-to-be.

While Baridine made his way towards them and Pettigis bowed and flattered, Orrie reached inside the back of Spin's gown, where a vent had been left for just this purpose, and made a couple of swift adjustments, working blind.

Then she stepped back, fading into the crowd.

Milandree nodded to Loar as she took up her position outside Lady Casillienne's chambers.

"Got the duty, did you?" Loar jerked his head at the door. "Hope you weren't expecting a present for it. She's as tight as a mouse's arse, that one. Can't be bothered with a good morning, never mind silver."

"Rather this than drunk guests."

"Oh, yeah, you had one last night, din't you? Lady Thingummy. Give you a 'present', did she?" He smirked.

Milandree stared ahead. "I don't tell tales."

"Hah. Too right. Least she's got no husband to make a fuss." Loar scratched his ear. "No such luck for me, haven't got your looks." He peered at her. "Mind, you're not looking your best. Up too late, were we?" He chuckled.

Milandree scowled, and rubbed at her eyes – carefully, so as not to disturb the shadows Alina had painted under them. "Feeling a bit off."

"Get some of the party leftovers, if they leave you any. Bit of cold goose, goes down a treat with some cabbage and taters, that. Where the hell's Badri and Chun, I want some beer before those bastards drink the lot."

The two new guards appeared moments later, wiping their mouths and looking sulky.

"There you are, you lazy fuckers," Loar said. "Right, well, you should have a quiet night, unless Herself decides to do a runner, eh? See you in the morning."

Chun made a crude joke. Badri barely acknowledged either Loar or Milandree, but slumped against the wall, and belched loudly.

Neither were drunk. That would have made things easier. They weren't particularly pleasant, but that didn't mean she wanted to damage them unnecessarily.

It felt close to midnight. A salty breeze whipped through the arrow-slits, making the torches flicker and dance. The castle thrummed with the wind. Milandree frowned. Alina could sail all right, but crossing the bay in this weather was going to be no fun at all.

Even assuming that everything else went to plan.

The wind hid the sound of footsteps, so Alina seemed to manifest at the end of the corridor silent as a ghost. Badri straightened.

"Oh, oh," Alina said, "please, sirs, I'm lost, I don't know where

I am, and my mistress is so sick, it's Thunder Fever, I'm sure of it..."

"What?" Both guards turned towards Alina, and Milandree moved.

Chun went down swiftly, the noise of his fall making Badri turn – too late to avoid Milandree's hold.

But he proved to have a thick and sturdy neck. It was also sweaty. Milandree cursed silently as Badri writhed in her grip, and barked out a cry. She tightened her hold, and he fell to his knees, bringing her down with him. She kept her knee in his spine, while Alina ran up to them, dropped to the floor, tore open a waxed parcel and clamped a pungent-smelling cloth over his nose.

He went rigid, then limp.

Milandree's vision blurred, and the floor of the corridor tilted under her. She saw, mistily, Alina apply the cloth to Chun, shove it back into its parcel and wrap it.

"Ooops. No you don't," Alina whispered, grabbing her arm. "Up with you."

Milandree scrambled to her feet, leaning on the wall. "Could have warned me."

"I could have said 'hold your breath' without him getting the idea?" Alina pressed her ear to the chamber door, and straightened. "Nothing." She looked at Badris. "That won't last long, we need to get him away out of sight. Where the fuck is Orrie?"

"Should have drawn her a map," Milandree said.

"Oh, never mind. I'll get on with the wards anyway." Alina drew a deep breath, and began a series of complex, somehow lacy gestures, muttering under her breath. Gritty smoke started to curl up around the doorframe.

"Orrivine! Orrivine!" Pettigis screamed.

"Let go! Let go of me!" Baridine roared.

Spin twirled gracefully about the floor, Lord Baridine held firmly, indeed inescapably, in its arms. He clutched at its waist to stay upright, his boots skidded and scraped as he tried to get purchase on the stones. The crowd moved in surges, trying to stay out of the way, but unwilling to leave such an astonishing spectacle. Among the shocked cries and helpful suggestions were unmistakable snickerings.

Word had spread, and the majority of the servants had gathered to witness this turn of events. There was a certain satisfaction on not a few faces, but others looked horrified. "It's a demon!" Someone shrieked.

"It's the goddess's vengeance, is what it is," someone muttered at the back of the crowd.

"Artisan!" Dowager Lady Baridine yelled. "Control that thing!"

Pettigis, swallowing, edged closer, and made vague gestures at the whirling couple.

"What are you doing, you useless creature? Help him!" Lady Baridine stepped down from the dais, cutting a swathe through the crowd. "You! Thing! Unhand my son!" Spin span on. Reel simply stood, its head slightly cocked, as though admiring the spectacle. Lord Baridine's face was now a disturbing shade of scarlet. A medal pinned to his coat flew off, gleaming in the light.

Members of the guard poured into the room, fighting their way through the crowd, to see their lord waltzing helplessly. One hefted an axe, but a look from the Lady Dowager froze him where he stood.

"Form a ring!" The captain ordered. "Keep it contained!"

The guard linked arms, and created a circle that gradually closed about the spinning pair.

Orrie hurried along another corridor, cursing. She was thoroughly lost. West wing, west wing...where the hells was the west wing? Looking out of the window was no help, the sun was long set and all that could be seen was howling darkness and the occasional flurry of white foam.

"Here, you! Ain't you the artisan? Your master's calling you!"

Bollocks. Orrie blinked at the guard. "What?"

"Your master wants you! Get to the ballroom before that uncanny piece of fuckery breaks his Lordship's neck!"

"Well where *is* the ballroom?" Orrie wailed.

"Oh for... *that* way, end of the passage, left, then right."

"Towards the West Wing?"

"The West Wing's the other *side* of the ballroom. Move yer arse, woman!"

Orrie ducked past him, muttering *bollocks bollocks bollocks* as she scuttled out of sight. She didn't dare go back through the ballroom, and obviously she was too recognisable anyway. She looked around frantically. A tapestry hung against one wall, shifting in the breeze, but even if she could get it down it would be too heavy and thick to wrap around her.

She could hear the shrieks and curses coming from the ballroom, and edged closer.

Every door was packed with servants, all trying to see what was going on. Orrie crept past them.

One woman had a savoury smelling basket over her arm, draped with a cloth. Orrie whipped the cloth away and wrapped it over her head.

A shawl made a makeshift skirt. If she kept to the shadows, it would have to do.

Bollocks, the ballroom was huge. Why did the gentry build such stupidly big rooms? What was the point of it, just to flounce about in overcomplicated clothes, chattering about inanities?

Orrie turned a corner and belted along an empty corridor she hoped led in the right direction. At the end was another passageway running crosswise. She peered about desperately, taking her spectacles off and cleaning them and putting them back on as though that might help. The wind whistled along the corridors, making the torches stream and smoke. She had almost given up when the wind dropped briefly. Orrie stood still, tilting her head.

A faint light, a low rhythmic chanting and a whiff of metal and spice – the smell of a magic working – drifted down the corridor. Orrie bolted towards it.

"Oh thank fuck," Alina said, her voice slightly muffled by her mask. "Did you get lost again?"

Orrie did not deign to answer, instead pulling on her own mask and whipping out her roll of tools. "Is the ward off?"

"Yes."

Orrie knelt in front of the lock. "Then get out of the light."

"Yes ma'am."

Milandree neatly tied and gagged both guards, and propped them against the wall, before pulling her scarf up over her face.

As Orrie still muttered over the lock, Madis, no longer looking so deathly and dressed in the plain gear of a lower servant, appeared around the corner. "How are we doing?"

"It's..." There was a *clank*. "Open," Orrie said.

Madis pulled a cloth over her mouth and nose.

"Careful," Alina whispered... "careful..."

They all stepped away from the door. Milandree picked up one of the guards' polearms and used the butt end to ease the door open.

The torch in the corridor cast a low, dancing light through the doorway. There was no lamp alight in the room, and of the fire, only the smell of smoke remained. A draught hissed through a broken corner of the shutters. Alina edged forward into the room, and jerked back with a hiss of surprise.

Lady Casillienne, lying propped against the pillows, stared at them, her pale blue eyes wide open. Madis was at the bed in an instant, a hand over the woman's mouth.

"We're not here to hurt you," Alina said. "Just need something of yours. 'Scuse me." She folded down the covers.

There was no visible reaction on the face of the lady except for a slight expansion of her pupils.

Madis let out a gasp of relief. There was the belt, cinched tightly over the woman's plain linen shift, the material bunching above and below. It was engraved with symbols that seemed, in the uncertain light, to shift and squirm.

The wind rose to a howl, rattling the shutters.

Alina's bag bulged and sloshed. The jar was rocking back and forth violently.

"Someone please give that thing some water, I can't afford to be distracted while I do this," Alina snapped.

Milandree looked around. "There's no ewer."

"There's a jug on the sill, use that," Madis said.

Orrie, ignoring them all, was studying the belt, muttering to herself. She shook out a soft leather roll onto the coverlet, and a dozen different picks and fine tools gleamed in their pockets.

Lady Casillienne's breathing sped up. "We're not here to hurt you," Madis said. "We're just going to take the belt."

A faint whine came from the back of the Lady's throat.

Milandree grabbed the jar, unscrewed the lid and splashed in some water from the jug.

There was a *foof,* and a crack. Milandree swore.

The jar fell to the boards, and split. Lying in the remnants was a glistening creature of eyes and gills and feelers, gasping, and slightly larger than the thing that had been in the jar. Milandree scooped it up, dropped it in the jug, put it on the chest at the foot of the bed, then left the room.

"Now can we get on?" Alina snapped.

"Wait."

"What?" They looked at each other. The voice had not come from any of them; it hissed like a wave dying on the sand.

Except for Orrie, who was examining the lock on the belt, and Lady Casillienne, who had moved nothing but her eyes, they turned to look at the jug. A faint greenish glow bloomed above it.

"Seriously?" Alina said. "*Now?*"

The voice had ripples in it, a breeze on a lake. "A little sea-water in the jug, a little worship from the servant's hall. Not enough. I need the sea. Return me to the sea."

"You're not a river god, are you?" Alina said. "Wait, you said, the servants..."

"This is not the time!" Madis said.

Milandree, meanwhile, dragged in both unconscious guards.

"Mil, check the window," Alina said.

She did. "The shutters are nailed over."

"We'll return you to the sea when we get out of here," Alina said. "Promise."

"Oh great," Madis said. "Well that's fifty gold I'll never see again."

Alina took up a position by the bed, ready to recite the spell.

"Wait," Orrie said, "we have a problem."

"What now?" Madis said.

Orrie sat back. "This is a deathlock."

"A what?"

"A deathlock. I've only ever seen one. It was taken off a woman who tried to escape from a harem. If it's not opened exactly right, it will send a knife into the lady's guts."

Lady Casillienne whined again. Madis lifted her hand from the woman's mouth.

"Was *that* what you were trying to tell us?"

There was no answer but that faint breathy sound.

"You can't speak?" Madis said.

"No," said a voice. "She cannot. She is bound. Like me. I know the stink of such things, it spreads like blood in the water."

Alina looked at the jar, and then at the belt. "You... what?"

"That thing around her, it binds her will. As mine was bound, when I was trapped."

"Oh," Alina said. "Oh, no." Her hands were clasped in front of her face, as though she were praying. "Oh, bollockry and arsecake."

"What is it?" Madis said.

"I should have guessed, I should have guessed from the spell structure, and from *her,* except it's only a theory, and it's completely... No one's..."

"Alina," Madis said. "Calm down. Talk."

"This belt – it's not a focus. It's a *lock*. It's a lock on her Adeptcy – on her entire *will*. That's why she can't speak, why she's... *fuck.*"

"Well now," Madis said, after a moment's appalled silence. "There's a pretty engagement gift. That whirlwind romance... It wasn't a romance at all, was it? It was a kidnapping. Lord Baridine gets a bride, and her dowry, and control of her lands, and anyone who knows her well and might get suspicious is safely tucked away in the North until the passes open. That would explain the new priest, too. Maybe the old one wouldn't have been prepared to wed them under these circumstances. I expect he's been retired."

"Never mind that," Alina said. "Do you know what this means?"

"What?"

"A lock on someone's will? On their Adeptcy? It's utterly forbidden by every law of the Adepts' Guild. That belt's probably the most illegal item in existence."

"Oh, goodie," Madis said. "So if we try to sell it on, we'll have the entire Guild on our necks. Besides..." She looked at Lady Casillienne and sighed. "We can't, can we? I mean, something like that..."

"No, we can't, I mean, look at her! You want it used on someone else?"

"Oh." Madis said. "Oh, well, that's a proper bastard." She rolled her shoulders. "Right. Orrie. You've worked this lock before?"

"One like it, yes."

"Successfully."

"Yes. Although you should be aware," Orrie said, polishing her glasses, "that it was not on the first try. And in that case, the wearer was already dead."

"All right." Madis leaned over the woman on the bed. "If you want us to try to get this thing off you," Madis said, "knowing the risks, make a sound."

The wind battered the shutters and set the lamp flickering. The glow from the god's jar pulsed.

Lady Casillienne whined. A single tear ran shimmering down her pale cheek.

Madis let out a breath.

"Alina, Orrie, go."

Alina jammed her fingers into her hair, and closed her eyes. "Right. All right. Here goes."

She took a deep breath, let it out, dropped her hands, and began to chant. The air thickened with the metal-spice smell of magic. The engravings on the belt began to shift and blur, and this time, it was no trick of the light.

Orrie took off her spectacles, and looked at Lady Casillienne. "Try not to move. Or breathe or digest vigorously." Then she sighed, cleaned her spectacles carefully, and replaced them. She chose a pick and got to work.

Spin, finally, had come to a halt, releasing Lord Baridine, red-faced, panting, and furious. A weeping, grovelling Pettigis, unassisted since the servants had all urgently found other jobs to do, had scrambled the Whirligigs back into their crates. "Take them away!" Baridine yelped. "I never want to see the things again!"

"Yes, my Lord, my Lord, I can't apologise enough, my apprentice, I..."

"Get out of my sight!"

"Yes, my Lord."

The Dowager Lady Baridine, after giving Pettigis a glare that promised disaster, had retreated to her chambers. Lord Baridine called for another jug of wine to calm his shattered nerves.

As he sat scowling, gulping, and wiping his face, the Captain of the Guard looked at him, and decided that he would handle the unfortunate matter of the Lady Tanisal himself, and inform his Lordship tomorrow, after the wedding, when his mood should have improved.

Four

Milandree assessed the water-gate, the prepared corpse draped unceremoniously over her shoulder. Three guards were playing cards at a table by the dock.

"Terrible night," one said.

"Awful." The second looked around, and made a surreptitious rocking gesture with one hand. "May Ilianu protect us."

The third made the same gesture, then looked shamefaced. "Don't let the Captain hear that," he said.

"Captain can go fuck a goose."

Milandree decided that was a good moment to make her presence felt. She coughed, hard and racking, and staggered towards them, the corpse lolling on her back.

"What the fuck?" The guards leapt to their feet, cards and tankards scattering.

"Got to get this off the Rock," she said. "Dead. Thunder Fever." And coughed again.

"Go, go!" Said one, waving at the dock. "Just take a boat."

"Waiting for her maid," Milandree rasped.

"Another one? Little gods. Right, lads, I think I hear the Captain calling," said the largest guard, who was already backing up the corridor.

"Do you?" Said another.

"Yes, he does," said the third. "We're urgently needed *somewhere else*." Grabbing the slower guard by the elbow, he marched him at speed up the corridor.

Then there was no one but Milandree, the corpse, and a number of boats tipping on the swell. Even here in the shelter of the dock, under the lee of Brute Rock, the boats were dancing. Milandree eyed them uneasily. Alina was a good sailor and she herself could handle a boat in a pinch, but the night was getting wilder by the moment. The wind roared in the Rock's throat like a vengeful spirit.

She picked a boat that two could handle, got the corpse on board, and settled herself to wait.

Orrie had stopped muttering. That was always a worrying moment. The only sounds were Alina's voice rising to the climax of the spell, the faint scratching of the lockpick, and the thrumming of the walls as the wind and sea raged. Even the little god seemed to be holding its breath.

A shudder of light rippled across the belt, and the symbols stopped moving – now all looking slightly different. Alina let out a huge breath and folded to her knees, her head hanging.

Lady Casillienne's eyes widened. Animation flooded into her face, like water rushing into a long-dry stream. Without looking up Orrie said; "Lady. Do. Not. Move."

The shadows on Lady Casillienne's throat shifted as she began to swallow, and stopped.

There was a click.

The belt opened.

Orrie sat back. "There," she said, and eased the belt out from under her.

Lady Casillienne stayed still for a moment, her eyes shifting towards Orrie, and the belt in her hands. Then she sat up, and raised her hands, and looked at them, and looked up at the masked women beside her bed. She straightened, and shifted her head on her neck, much like an eagle that has just spotted its prey. Those pale blue eyes, now the life was back in them, were disturbingly sharp.

Madis opened the door. "They're about to change the guard...Oh."

Lady Casillienne looked at her. "Get me out of here," she said, "and I'll triple whatever you expected to get for the belt."

"Right you are," Madis said. "Alina. Alina!" She helped Alina to her feet. "Can you run?"

"I can try," Alina rasped. "Gods, that was... Lady? Are you..."

"I am well," Lady Casillienne said, "but my Adeptcy... I can't feel it. Let us hope it returns."

"Let's hope," Madis said. "Alina, go. Get to the boat."

"But what about..." Alina said.

"We'll manage. Now *move* – the guard's about to change, I heard the order."

Alina staggered for the door, turned back, and scooped the jug from the dresser. "Promised," she said, and stumbled out of the room.

"Orrie?" Madis said. "We need to change things slightly."

Orrie looked at Madis, and at Lady Casillienne, and sighed. "Right. I'll meet you later."

"Try not to get lost, all right? Now, Your Ladyship," Madis said, "I suggest we get you into one of these guards' uniforms. Fast."

"You think that will work?" Lady Casillienne said.

"Not for long. But with luck, for long enough."

Milandree spotted Alina weaving down the passageway. She glanced over her shoulder. Outside, the wind had gone from vengeful spirit to a whole graveyard of them.

She leapt over the side and scooped Alina bodily into the boat. "What in the name of..."

"Spell. Stronger than I thought. Oh, my *head.*" Alina put the jug she was clutching on the boards with a shaking hand. "Cast... cast off." She put her hands over her eyes.

Milandree cast off. The boat began to drift sideways. "Alina. Alina! We need to get out of here. Tell me what to do."

Alina stared blearily into the roaring dark. "It's all rocking." She crumpled to the deck in a dead faint.

"Oh, crap," Milandree said.

"Put me in the sea," said the voice from the jug.

"What?" Milandree was looking around desperately. She wasn't a good enough sailor to take the boat out without Alina, not in this weather, and there was nowhere else to go but back into the castle, where they were more likely than not to run into the guard heading to the dock to stop them.

That option was rapidly disappearing as the dock retreated, and the large boat on which most of the guests had arrived loomed nearer.

"Put me in the sea."

"We're about to hit that ship! We'll drown and you'll get crushed!"

Something like a laugh bubbled out of the jug. "No. You think it was the Sky God turned this Brute to Brute Rock? It was not. It was I. It was Ilianu. Put me back where I belong."

Distracted, barely listening, Milandree said, "Fine, fine. Here you go. Bye." She tipped the jug over the side, and bent over Alina.

Only her superb reflexes saved her from falling on top of the unconscious woman as the little boat suddenly rose and surged forward, borne towards the entrance of the dock at frightening speed, and against the wind. Spray plumed over the bow. Milandree swore, wrapped one arm around the mast and the other around Alina, and held on for both their lives.

Alina coughed, spat and shook wet locks out of her eyes. "Milandree?" She sat up and gaped. "What..."

"You all right?"

"Better. Wet. Wait. Milandree? The sail... the sail's not set. How are we moving?"

"Brace yourself." Milandree helped her to her feet. "And hold on."

The little boat was scudding across the bay. The storm had lessened, but all around the waves still billowed and danced. The painter stretched from the bow into the water before them, thrumming with tension. Alina blinked at it. "Are we..." She stumbled back as something huge and sleekly dark breached alongside the boat, foam running pale down its sides.

"Escort," Milandree said. "That little god? Not so little."

"Oh, I meant to put it in the..." Alina broke off. "She was Ilianu, wasn't she? Goddess of Quat Bay. I thought, when she said about worship from the servants, but..." After a moment, she whispered, "How in the name of *anything* did she end up in a jar on a market stall?"

Milandree gave her a straight stare. "Didn't seem prudent to ask."

"Ah. Maybe not. So... are we still going to make our landing?"

"Told her where we wanted to go. Are we going there?"

Alina pulled a compass from her pocket, and squinted. "Probably? We're headed for the shore, at any rate." She looked out at the tumultuous darkness, and ran her hands through her sopping hair. "Is there any food on this boat?"

Dawn was a stormy yellow streak on the horizon. Milandree and Alina watched as the quay came in sight. As they drew near, the painter went slack.

Alina grabbed it and called "Thank you."

A flip of a gigantic tail drenched them with spray, and then their escort was gone.

"I *was* beginning to dry out," Milandree said.

"Don't be ungrateful."

They bumped against the quay, deserted at this hour. Alina jumped ashore with the painter, and secured the boat.

Milandree followed, lifting out the now slightly damp corpse.

"Ladies," said a voice.

Arden, accompanied by three men, less elegantly dressed but bearing identical, smug grins, appeared on the quay. "Please step aside."

"Oh you're *joking,*" Alina groaned.

Milandree said nothing, though there were enough daggers in her look to puncture an army.

"I'm really not," Arden said, still smiling. "Ah, I believe this scowling... fellow... must be the famous Milandree. Now, my companions – not to mention myself – are *real* swordsmen. Will you let us take the prize without forcing us to be ungentlemanly?"

Milandree looked at the men, and at Alina, and shook her head.

"I'm a fool to ask, but will we at least get the half you promised?" Alina said, shaking water out of her skirts.

"Allowing the prize to be taken at this juncture proves that dear

Madis is not the thief she thinks she is," Arden said. "I *really* don't feel she's earned it, and therefore, neither have you. I assume she at least arranged transport for you, so we will take our leave before it turns up." He gestured his men to pick up the corpse, swept them a bow, and left.

"Well," Alina said. "That's that." She wrapped her arms around herself. "Where in all the hells is Dagri? I'm freezing."

Madis only stared into the night, where Arden and his men had disappeared.

"What do you mean she's *gone?* Where the hells is she?" Lord Baridine hissed.

The guard shook his head. "She can't have left the castle, Milord, unless..." his heavy face suddenly grew waxy with discomfort.

"Unless what?"

"The boat, Milord. The unfortunate Lady Tanisal. Last night. If you remember..."

"But... wait... you think she could have got on that boat? With the corpse? Wasn't it searched?"

The guard, beginning to sweat, shook his head. "There was no reason to, My Lord. No one had any idea she might try to... I mean, that anyone would attempt a kidnapping! And besides, the fever..."

"Fuck the fever! Send out boats! Get men after them!"

"At once, My Lord." The guard bolted from the chamber, boots ringing on the stone.

"The rest of you, search the castle!" Lord Baridine shouted. "Not one guest is to leave until everything's been checked, bag, baggage and underwear, you understand me?"

"My Lord!"

"Wait!" The Dowager's voice cracked over them like a whip, stopping the rush.

"Mother..."

"My boy, *think.*" She grabbed his elbow, pulling him close, and hissed in his ear. "If she has got away, and someone manages to get that belt off without killing her, you're going to need every ally you can scrape up. And most of them are here. Any search must be discreet, and polite, and," she gripped harder, making him wince, "driven by *concern* for your bride-to-be, who has been *behaving strangely,* and may be *under some magical influence."*

"But isn't that..." Baridine stopped at her glare.

"A lie laced with truth is a deal easier to swallow. It leaves us room to turn this to our advantage." She turned to the guard, and raised her voice. "Lady Casillienne is to be found and safely detained. Anyone with her may be the person who is kidnapping her and should be captured if possible, killed if not. Tell the guests there's a rogue Adept at loose, and make sure they're kept in their rooms. Search the boats first, then the rooms of each party of guests. Count how many people are in each party and how many pieces of luggage they have big enough to hold a body. Once they've been searched, escort them to the boats. But if there is a single extra person, a single extra box, stop them, and check. All this is to be done with *every possible courtesy."*

Baridine pulled out of her grip. "You heard the Dowager," he snapped. "Get to it."

Orrie bent her head and carried on packing straw around the Whirligigs as Pettigis, grey with hangover and bile, ranted about the room, waving his hands. "Ruined! I'm *ruined!* I should never have let you talk me into using those things, you *wretched* girl! Oh, my name, my reputation, I shall have to leave the city, I shall have to go to some wretched country town where no one can make a decent coat, I shall have to mend watches for peasants! It's all your fault! After everything I've done for you... why are we even *taking* those horrible things?"

As he seemed to be pausing for breath, Orrie pushed her glasses up on her nose and said, "Leaving them here might remind his Lordship of the... incident. And they contain valuable materials that can be re-used. Or sold."

"Oh, very well, very well. I shall need every penny since that wretched woman died before she could pay me for them! The minute we get back your apprenticeship is *over,* you understand. As soon as you've chased her estate for the money."

"Yes, Master Pettigis."

"And written letters of apology to Lord Baridine, and the new Lady Baridine, and the Dowager."

"Yes, Master Pettigis."

"And make it absolutely clear that while I was responsible for their... that you... that it was your meddling that set things on such a course! If you'd left my creations alone, they would have been perfectly fine!"

Orrie blinked, and concentrated very hard on the crate. "Yes, Master Pettigis," she said, her voice as carefully colourless as her clothes.

"Artisan! Open up, by order of his Lordship!"

Pettigis' grey complexion gained a greenish cast as the guard hammered on the door. "A moment, a moment!" He looked around frantically and then shoved Orrie in front of him. "She's the one you want!" He opened the door, and two guards blinked down at Orrie, who blinked up.

"Um, no, she isn't," one said. "We're looking for Lady Casillienne. She... uh..."

"Her Ladyship is not herself and may be under magical influence," the other guard said. "She's not in her chambers. We're searching the castle. For her own safety. And there's a rogue Adept."

"A *dangerous* rogue Adept," the other guard added. "So you've to stay in your rooms until you're escorted to the boats. For safety."

"Well Lady Casillienne isn't here!" Pettigis said. "But of course, please, do search, and do tell his Lordship I was *entirely* willing to help, and anything I can do..." He babbled on as the guard poked about the room, wincing as they tugged several fancy shirts from his trunk. Orrie winced in turn as they rummaged through a box of tools in which nothing bigger than a fairly small cat would have fitted, sending several clattering to the floor.

Finally they came to the Whirligigs. The guards looked at them, and then at each other. "Have to ask you to open them up," said one, holding his spear at the ready – perhaps in case Spin decided to grasp him in the same embrace his Lordship had endured.

"Open them..." Pettigis said. "But why?"

"Well, could be someone hiding inside," the guard said.

Orrie looked at the Whirligigs, then at the guards. "Um," she said. "There isn't room."

"Open 'em." The guard growled.

"If you insist. But you see, the mechanism..." Orrie unhinged the face of Reel, and swung it open, revealing a pair of blue-glass eyes hanging disconcertingly amid a series of levers and wheels, "it fills the whole shell." She left the face open, and moved to the torso. "You see the cogs here, they turn this reticulating arm, here, which extends down..." Larger wheels and levers filled the torso. Orrie embarked on a lengthy discussion of how each cog and lever connected to each, gesturing so enthusiastically with the screwdriver she held that she narrowly missed whacking one of the guards on the leg. "And you see this bit here? That's the ultimator. It works by reversing the motion of the diticulating wheel..." She opened the lower half – "Which attaches in there, behind all those cogs."

A mass of tiny wheels filled the opening. "Now *this* one connects to the..."

"Never mind!" The guard said. "The other one!"

"Oh, it's the same, but with slight adjustments for the difference in weight," Orrie leapt towards Spin waving her screwdriver, and opened the face. "Let me show you. It's actually fascinating, you see here where the balancing lever..."

"Yes, well, that will do, never mind," the guard said. "His Lordship asks that you stay in here until the boats are ready."

A boatful of Baridine Castle Guard bumped into Quat Quay, and scrambled out, leading their horses. "Here, you!" The Captain waved at the nearest person, a woman in an embroidered jacket and leather trousers, leaning on a bollard in the sun, cleaning a piece of tack. "We're seeking some people who came in at dawn," the Captain said. "A man, a woman, and... well, a dead woman. Did you see anything?"

"Oh, yes, the poor dead lady," she said. "Picked her up and just slung her on a horse. Most impious. Went that way, up the sheep track."

"After them!"

As the guards made their way up the track, four riderless horses trotted past them. The one in the lead was a magnificent animal, with an arched neck and dappled flanks, which a certain Lord Galzas might, if it had still had a white blaze, have recognised.

"Should we..."

"Ignore them," the Captain snapped. "Wait, what's that up ahead?"

A small boy was waving his hands above his head. "This way! This way!" He pointed up a side-track.

"What's up there?" the Captain said.

"Are you the constables?"

"No."

"Oh. Thought you were. They found a dead woman!" The boy's face was alight with excitement. "It's *awful.*"

The guards looked at each other, and made their way up the path.

Just over the brow of the hill was a small, tumbledown shelter. A group of people were gathered about it. From their dress, they were fishers, farmers, and traders, who had been on their way to or from the quay. They seemed extremely agitated.

In their midst, firmly held by a number of brawny arms and guarded with two shovels, three pitchforks and a large hammer, were three men, one of them dressed extravagantly in a green velvet coat with gold buttons.

None of them were the lady's maid or the absent guard.

"What's going on here?" The Captain said.

"Desecration!" said an ancient man, sucking his remaining tooth for emphasis. "The poor lady!" He jerked his head towards the shelter.

A corpse lay on the earthen floor. By her dress, it was definitely the one they were looking for. But Thunder Fever, though it had many unpleasant effects, had not done this. Even in the low light of the shelter it was obvious the unfortunate woman had been opened up from gullet to garters.

The Captain stared at the body. It had been a while since he'd seen combat, but he was *fairly* certain that a corpse usually had more blood in it. And innards. But then, she had been dead before she left the Rock. Perhaps that happened when someone died of the Thunder Fever. Such mysteries were best left for those who got paid to deal with them. He backed out, feeling even more confused, and somewhat sick.

"They gutted her like a fish!" said one man. "He had his hands in her up to the elbows! If something hadn't spooked their horses, so they come racing out, all of a lather, just as Forber and me were passing, they'd have got clean away!"

"Something?" One of the detained men choked. "It was that demon in horse form, that's what you should be after, it ripped their tethers right apart, and drove them down the track, it's a demon, I tell you!"

It was true that fragments of leather, bearing what looked a great deal like the marks of horse teeth, still hung from a nearby tree.

"Demon! Hah! Horses know," said a woman with a basket of carrots, nodding with pursed lips. "They can smell evil, horses. They chewed through their own tethers to get away from you!"

"It was that demon horse, I tell you!"

"Oh, do shut up," said the man in the green velvet coat. "You really aren't helping."

"Here, you," the Captain said. "There were two others with her. A man and a woman. What happened to them?"

"Two more?" Growled the man with the hammer. "Hah, I'll bet they murdered them too!"

"I didn't murder anybody!" The green-velvet-coat man said. "It must have been my... them! Those others! They killed her! I just... We found the lady and thought perhaps she might be revived..."

"Liar! Murderer!"

The Captain, realising that his quarry was long gone, and that this fancy-dressed degenerate was no business of his, beckoned his men and headed back to the quay, mentally preparing his excuses for the Dowager.

Behind them, the shouting continued until the town constables arrived.

After a few hours and a deal of vituperation and wailing from Pettigis, news came through that the hunt for Lady Casillienne had failed. The guests, most now torn between annoyance at the high-handed way they had been dealt with, irritation at the cancellation of the wedding, and the delightful possibilities for gossip and intrigue suggested by the bride's disappearance, were permitted to leave the Rock.

Orrie struggled the two wheeled boxes containing the Whirligigs into the corridor. Pettigis, burdened only with a small bag of clothes and his self-pity, had already left for the boat.

A passing guard gallantly took one of the boxes, and they steered them towards the dock.

In the room she had just left, an old coat lay abandoned in one corner. Spilling out from beneath it were a number of cogs, wheels and levers, apparently forgotten in the artisans' haste to pack.

Dagri jumped down from her perch on the quay when Shaikan appeared, with the three riderless horses in tow. Milandree and Alina emerged from the shed behind her. "That horse is positively uncanny," Alina said.

Shaikan snorted, and spat out a fragment of leather.

The three of them mounted up, and headed back to town, the remaining horse trotting behind.

Orrie unloaded the cart as Pettigis secluded himself in his office, drinking heavily and beginning and discarding a dozen letters of exculpation and excuse to Lord Baridine, Lady Baridine, and all of the guests. He appeared to have forgotten he had told Orrie to do it.

She manoeuvred the two cases around to the back of the shop, checked that no one was in earshot, and unlocked the bell-shaped lower half of each Whirligig.

Two figures crumpled out onto the floor, accompanied by a clatter of cogwheels all wired together into the thin but effective sheets that had been hanging inside the openings.

"Aagh," Madis said. "I'll never move again. My *knees.*"

Lady Casillienne, still in her guards' uniform, only groaned.

It did not, however, escape her notice that Madis now wore, as well as her guard's uniform, two ropes of pearls, a rather good set of emeralds, and a large ruby ring.

The small boarding house still smelled of cheap stew and damp. The fellow who opened the door to the party was as colourless as ever, though his sandy eyebrows rose a little at the sight of the heavily cloaked women on his doorstep. "Help you?"

One of the women pushed past him, shouting, "Deanna! Deanna!"

With a clatter of boots the woman who had hired Arden to steal the belt came running down the stairs, pausing at the bottom, open mouthed. "My Lady!"

"None of that, my dear, we're among friends here." Lady

Casillienne held out her hands. "Deanna."

"Oh dear gods," the woman said, and flung herself into Lady Casillienne's arms. "You're safe, you're safe, I thought... I didn't..."

"Deanna." Lady Casillienne hugged her hard, closing her eyes. "I thought they'd killed you."

"The others... they killed the others. I hid in a ditch, I..." her breath hitched. "Thoma fell on top of me, dead. Hid me. I heard them talking as they put the belt on you. Waited. When they were gone, I climbed out. I couldn't get word home, couldn't trust anyone would believe me in a place where the Baridines have so many supporters so... I hired a thief to steal the belt. I believed once it was off you would find a way..." she shook her head, and swallowed.

Lady Casillienne lifted her head, and released her friend. "That is why you are my closest advisor, Deanna." Her gaze hardened. "And why you will help me devise an appropriate response to what the Baridines tried to do to me."

"Are you... Did it..." Deanna stammered.

"My Adeptcy is returning, slowly."

"Thank the gods. But where is the man I hired?" Deanna said. "And who are these ladies?"

"I have no idea who you hired, but these are my rescuers."

Madis bowed. "Ma'am. The man you hired, hired us. He... Well, let's just say he was about as trustworthy as the Baridines. In any case, I'm glad to see you safely reunited."

"What happened to the belt?" Deanna said.

"I've got it," Alina said, patting her bag. "I didn't dare let it out of my sight."

"You didn't *wear* it?"

"Ugh, no, I wrapped it in every binding I could come up with on short notice and shoved it in my bag. It should be destroyed, but I'm not sure how to do it safely."

"I suggest," Lady Casillienne said, "you take it to the Adepts' Guild. With a letter I shall provide, under my seal. I shall also provide the full Guild fee – the standard fee, not the ridiculous one they wish you to pay."

"My Lady?" Alina said.

"You wish to join them, do you not? I will suggest, strongly, that you are allowed to do so, and to progress to full Guild status, like anyone else, and in return *I* will refrain from mentioning to his Majesty, under whose licence the Guild exists, that the Adepts' Guild somehow permitted the creation of such an incredibly dangerous item, and its use against the leader of a *currently* friendly foreign power." Lady Casillienne smiled. It was warm, genuine, and utterly remorseless.

Alina stared, then squeaked. "*Thank* you!"

"In the meantime," Lady Casillienne continued, "I have access to banking facilities in Brisha. I will pay you, as promised, three times what you were offered." She hesitated. "Deanna, you *do* still have my seal?"

"Yes."

"That's a relief." She looked at Milandree. "I shall hire guards, also. I don't plan to make my presence here public, but Baridine might yet come looking. I'll also need an escort once the passes open. As you know the local area I would appreciate your advice on that."

"Ma'am." Milandree said.

"I will need someone to train my new personal guard. Mine were good people," grief darkened her face for a moment, "but it seems, not good enough. Might you be interested in such a thing? A temporary position, at least to begin with."

"I..." Milandree blinked. "Ma'am. I mean, yes, ma'am. Thank you."

"I could use a good artisan, too," she said, looking at Orrie. "Even in my condition, I was impressed by your Whirligigs."

"Um." Orrie blinked. "Thank you. Only... I have something I have to do. For someone."

"Of course. Well, for the future, the offer remains. If I can assist with what you plan, assuming it is legal..." the merest fragment of a smile brushed her mouth, "please inform me."

Finally, she turned to Madis. The two women regarded each other with cool interest until Madis' own mouth quirked upwards. "Ma'am?"

Lady Casillienne tapped the side of her mouth with one forefinger. "I find myself tempted to create a position of First Thief of the Household, purely for you, but you would not take it."

"No, ma'am, thank you all the same."

"You will of course be paid. But you – all of you," she swept them with her glance – "freed me from…" Her control flickered, and her eyes were for a moment those of an animal in a snare, who hears the tread of the hunter. Then the look was gone as though it had never been. "Not just me, but my people. What that man would have left of my poor country, when he had done with it, I can hardly bear to imagine. Money is a useful thing, but should any of you, in future, need help that money alone cannot provide, I ask you to call on me. Discreetly, of course."

Five

A few weeks later there was a meeting at the Black Pig. There was pie, and beer, and wine, and a great deal of merriment. Nib fell asleep on her mother's lap.

"So," Alina said, over her daughter's lolling head. "Did you hear? Baridine entered the Stone Order!"

"The Stone Order?" Madis almost choked on her beer. "Aren't they one of those raw-roots and silent contemplation lot? He won't last a week!"

Alina beamed. "After all the money he poured into the wedding that never was, his creditors got *really* narky. His mother's retiring to the dower house, which, my loves, is not only in a *very* damp and unfashionable patch of the remaining family lands but has been horribly neglected for years – presumably because she didn't ever plan to live there."

"They're lucky Her Ladyship didn't have 'em both assassinated," Madis said. "Frankly, I probably would have. On the other hand, her way, they both live in misery for as long as their health holds up, and neither of them dare complain, in case the truth comes out." She frowned at her beer. "I tell you what – I'm glad she owes us."

"You should be," Milandree said. "Baridine gifted her Brute Rock."

They looked at each other for a long moment, as the implications sank in.

"Can he *do* that?" Orrie said.

"It was crown gift, free, clear, unentailed. He can do what he likes with it." Milandree gave one of her rare smiles. "Don't suppose he *did* like it, but he's done it."

"Bloody *hells,*" Madis said. "So Lady Casillienne now controls the most strategically important stronghold on this entire coast."

"Yep." Milandree frankly grinned.

"You like her!" Alina accused.

"Admire," Milandree said. "Don't you?"

"Oh, definitely." Alina stroked Nib's curls. "Admire. Am frankly slightly terrified of. Basically, she's an enemy I *really* don't want. Speaking of things I don't want, Madis, what happened to your wretched brother?"

"He's in jail. They couldn't prove murder, so he got done for desecration of a body." She smiled. "I thought of breaking him out, just to annoy him, but I decided a few months of bad food and no change of clothes will do him good."

"How long do you think it took him to realise we knew he was listening, at the Black Pig?"

"Who knows?" Madis snorted. "He may not yet. He *really* isn't as smart as he thinks he is."

"He won't change, you know," Alina said.

"I know."

Alina shifted Nib's weight. "So Milandree's off to Darnor to train guards, I'm starting my apprenticeship in three days, what about you, Orrie?"

"I'm taking Enlarius to Tessery." She pushed her glasses up on her nose, and lifted her tankard. "Here's to flying pigs, eh?"

"Dagri?"

"I am looking for a mare for Shaikan. I think I have found one, but obtaining her will take work."

"And you, Madis?" Alina's mouth drooped. "I feel as though we're all abandoning you."

"Pah. You'll finish your apprenticeship at top speed, Milandree will get fed up of the Northern winters, and Whassname of Tessery won't want to keep Ollie around once he knows she's a better Artificer without Adeptcy than he is with it. In the meantime," Madis grinned. "That mare Dagri wants is currently the most prized possession of the Caliph of Ibarian. We're going to steal her."

She raised her tankard. "Cheers."

About the Author

Gaie Sebold's debut novel introduced brothel-owning ex-avatar of sex and war, *Babylon Steel* (Solaris, 2012); followed by the sequel, *Dangerous Gifts*. The steampunk fantasy *Shanghai Sparrow* came out in 2014 and *Sparrow Falling* in 2016. Her stories have appeared in a number of magazines and anthologies, including the BFS Award shortlisted anthology *Fight Like a Girl*. She is a freelance copy editor, runs writing workshops, grows vegetables, and was a judge for the 2017 Arthur C Clarke Award.

Her website is www.gaiesebold.com and you can find her on twitter @GaieSebold

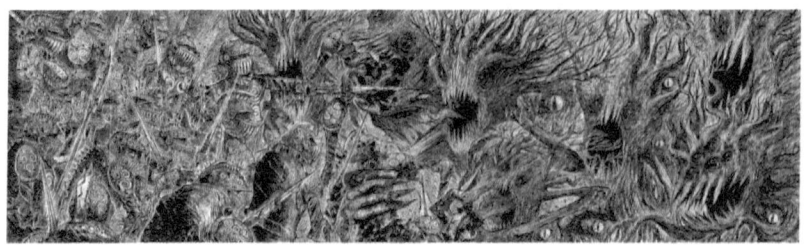

NewCon Press Novella Set 6: Blood and Blade

Four stand-alone novellas of sword play, sorcery, blood-drenched battles, noble deeds and fool-hardy endeavours, linked only by their shared cover art. Released summer 2019, in paperback, limited edition hardback, and as a slipcased set featuring all four novellas as signed hardbacks and **Duncan Kay**'s combined artwork as a wrap-around.

In **Edward Cox**'s *The Bone Shaker,* Sir Vladisal and her knights are lost within endless woodlands. Harried by demons, they seek the kidnapped son of their Duchess, facing terror at every turn. **Gaie Sebold** takes us on *A Hazardous Engagement,* wherein a wily gang of thieves are set an impossible task.

Fortunately, they never know when to quit. In *Serpent Rose,* **Kari Sperring** takes us to the realm of Avalon and the intrigues surrounding some of the lesser known knights and characters of King Arthur's court, while in **Gavin Smith**'s *Chivalry* we follow a young knight from the tourney fields to the battlefield, where he is forced to grow up rapidly as he faces challenges beyond his wildest imaginings.

Four stunning tales of epic fantasy scaled down to novella size by four outstanding authors.

More New Titles from NewCon Press

David Gullen – Shopocalypse

A Bonnie and Clyde for the Trump era, Josie and Novik embark on the ultimate roadtrip. In a near-future re-sculpted politically and geographically by climate change, they blaze a trail across the shopping malls of America in a printed intelligent car (stolen by accident), with a hundred and ninety million LSD-contaminated dollars in the trunk, buying shoes and cameras to change the world.

Kim Lakin-Smith – Rise

Charged with crimes against the state, Kali Titian (pilot, soldier, and engineer), is sentenced to Erbärmlich prison camp, where few survive for long. Here she encounters Mohab, the Speaker's son, and uncovers two ancient energy sources, which may just bring redemption to an oppressed people. The author of *Cyber Circus* returns with a dazzling tale of courage against the odds and the power of hope.

Andrew Wallace – Celebrity Werewolf

Suave, sophisticated, erudite and charming, Gig Danvers seems too good to be true. Appearing from nowhere, he champions humanitarian causes and revolutionises science,developing the first organic computer to exceed silicon capacity; but are his critics right to be cautious? Is there a darker side to this enigmatic benefactor, one that is more in keeping with his status as the Celebrity Werewolf?

Legends 3 – edited by Ian Whates

David Gemmell passed away in 2006, leaving behind a legacy of memorable characters, and thrilling tales. The *Legends* series of anthologies, of which this the third and almost certainly final volume, is intended to pay homage to one of fantasy fiction's greatest writers. Features a selection of dazzling stories written especially for the books by some of the finest fantasy authors around.

www.newconpress.co.uk

IMMANION PRESS
Purveyors of Speculative Fiction

Strindberg's Ghost Sonata & Other Uncollected Tales by Tanith Lee

This book is the first of three anthologies to be published by Immanion Press that will showcase some of Tanith Lee's most sought-after tales. Spanning the genres of horror and fantasy, upon vivid and mysterious worlds, the book includes a story that has never been published before – 'Iron City' – as well as two tales set in the Flat Earth mythos; 'The Pain of Glass' and 'The Origin of Snow', the latter of which only ever appeared briefly on the author's web site. This collection presents a jewel casket of twenty stories, and even to the most avid fan of Tanith Lee will contain gems they've not read before. ISBN 978-1-912815-00-5, £12.99, $18.99 pbk

A Raven Bound with Lilies by Storm Constantine

The Wraeththu have captivated readers for three decades. This anthology of 15 tales collects all the published Wraeththu short stories into one volume, and also includes extra material, including the author's first explorations of the androgynous race. The tales range from the 'creation story' *Paragenesis*, through the bloody, brutal rise of the earliest tribes, and on into a future, where strange mutations are starting to emerge from hidden corners of the earth. ISBN: 978-1-907737-80-0 £11.99, $15.50 pbk

The Lord of the Looking Glass by Fiona McGavin

The author has an extraordinary talent for taking genre tropes and turning them around into something completely new, playing deftly with topsy-turvy relationships between supernatural creatures and people of the real world. 'Post Garden Centre Blues' reveals an unusual relationship between taker and taken in a twist of the changeling myth. 'A Tale from the End of the World' takes the reader into her developing mythos of a post-apocalyptic world, which is bizarre, Gothic and steampunk all at once. 'Magpie' features a girl scavenging from the dead on a battlefield, whose callous greed invokes a dire curse. Following in the tradition of exemplary short story writers like Tanith Lee and Liz Williams, Fiona has a vivid style of writing that brings intriguing new visions to fantasy, horror and science fiction. ISBN: 978-1-907737-99-2, £11.99, $17.50 pbk

www.immanion-press.com
info@immanion-press.com